RETRIBUTION!

Mary Calvin sits in her flat for hours, full of fury and sick with despair for the dreadful waste of her friend's young life, Evelyn Torrance. A dreadful resolution begins to dominate her mind: retribution! Fred Tanner must pay for his crime! She takes sleeping tablets from the medicine chest and selecting a sharp ornamental dagger from the mantelshelf, she slips them into her handbag. She puts on her coat, hurries out and heads for Tanner's flat . . .

NORMAN LAZENBY

RETRIBUTION!

Complete and Unabridged

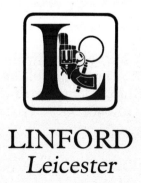

LINFORD
Leicester

First published in Great Britain

First Linford Edition
published 2012

British Library CIP Data

Lazenby, Norman A. (Norman Austin)
Retribution!.- -
(Linford mystery library)
1. Detective and mystery stories.
2. Large type books.
I. Title II. Series
813.5′4–dc23

ISBN 978–1–4448–0997–8

Published by
F. A. Thorpe (Publishing)
Anstey, Leicestershire

Set by Words & Graphics Ltd.
Anstey, Leicestershire
Printed and bound in Great Britain by
T. J. International Ltd., Padstow, Cornwall

This book is printed on acid-free paper

Part 1

Retribution!

1

Murder on her Mind

'You're a murderer! You should be hanged!' Mary Calvin shouted across the flat to him.

Fred Tanner laughed contemptuously, and leaned back in his armchair. His eyes mocked her through the cloud of smoke, which he coolly exhaled.

'Mary, you are very amusing. Just because a foolish girl decides to take her life, must you assume that I am responsible?'

Mary Calvin walked grimly across the apartment, a newspaper crushed in her hand.

'Evelyn Torrance took her life because she couldn't bear the shame of what was going to happen to her — and you were responsible! A lot of people know the truth. Aren't you afraid someone will kill you some day?'

'What rubbish you talk, Mary. Sit down and give me a little kiss.'

He laughed in her face as she stopped, and stared at him furiously.

'I simply loathe you!' Mary trembled with the intensity of her emotions. 'Evelyn was my friend, and you killed her. I wish I could kill you!'

'Dear me, did you drop in just to have hysterics, Mary? How disappointing. I should expect nicer behaviour from a lovely girl like you. I've always admired you, Mary.'

His liquid brown eyes, and handsome face were mocking her again.

'I know that Evelyn was not the only girl to make a fool of herself over you,' said Mary bitterly.

'I've always found the opposite sex very fascinating,' he acknowledged lazily.

He rose to his feet with nonchalant ease. He was tall, thin-waisted, and his well-tailored chalk-stripe suit fitted him like a glove. He strolled over to the girl, hands in pockets, a mocking smile on his face.

'You will not be returning to your little

hat shop tonight, my dear,' he said smoothly, 'so why not stay a little longer and have a drink with me?'

Mary Calvin nearly struck him with her clenched fist, but she stopped herself with an effort. White-faced and furious she stared at him. She was near to hysteria and with difficulty retained her composure. He glanced at her quizzically, wondering what was on her mind.

To Mary, at this moment, it seemed fantastic that he should speak the very words that would give her the chance to avenge Evelyn Torrance. Did he not guess why she had visited his rooms? Did he not know what lay concealed in her handbag?

She had sat for hours in her flat that fatal evening, full of fury and a sick despair for the dreadful waste of Evelyn Torrance's young life. One fact had emerged crystal clear in her mind; Fred Tanner must pay for his crime! She had acted with a dreadful resolution, surprising to herself. First, she took from the medicine chest a small bottle of sleeping tablets, which had lain there almost forgotten since her mother's last illness. Then she selected from the mantelshelf a sharp ornamental dagger, whose keen point she tested, then smiled, balancing the dagger on her hand. Next she put the tablets and weapon in her handbag, donned her coat and gloves, and hurried out.

'I think I'll have a drink now, as you suggest,' she heard herself saying.

She had known Fred Tanner would be drinking: he was a habitual drinker. She had known this from her few meetings with him. That was why she had brought the tablets. Outwardly she was calm. Yet in her mind she was convinced that her intentions screamed aloud to Tanner; but he walked out to the sideboard with a confident, sardonic air.

He returned with two glasses of whisky.

'I'm afraid I omitted to order cocktails, but then I hardly expected this — um — charming visit. Drink, my dear Mary. You will find life is not so confoundedly grim as you try to make out. Evelyn was a fool to take her life.'

She nearly threw the liquid in his

mocking face. Instead she tremblingly lifted the glass to her lips.

The whisky gave her courage, enabled her to see fiercely and clearly. She felt she hated Tanner more than ever. She sat on the arm of a chair, and he came nearer to her, an interrogative, leering expression on his face.

'I thought your temper would evaporate, Mary. Why the devil should we quarrel? Let's forget everything.'

'Could I have another drink?'

He glanced with mild surprise at her empty glass. He took the glass from her hand.

'Sure. I've got a bottle.' He put his half-empty glass down on the chair arm and turned away to the sideboard.

The small bottle was hidden in her hand. She acted under a fierce, impelling urge. She dropped three of the small pellets into the liquid, and watched them, fascinated, as they quickly dissolved in small bubbling fountains in the amber spirit.

Tanner returned, sauntering over with her glass.

'To our new friendship!' he boasted, and drank his whisky off with a gulp. He moved across the room again to replenish his glass. He looked twice at the empty glass, as if puzzled at the odd taste of the liquid. Then, with full glass again, he came back and bent his head near to hers. His arm went round her shoulders.

'I knew you couldn't be angry with me, Mary,' he said foolishly.

Grimly she marvelled at his enormous conceit. She sat stiffly, loathing the man. He rambled on with foolish talk, obsessed with the idea of an easy conquest. The girl watched him closely. She did not speak or move. Somewhere a clock struck the hour, and upon its very note, as upon a summons, Tanner's words suddenly became slurred. He staggered to a chair, staring in drowsy bewilderment. A moment later his eyes closed, and he fell into deep sleep, his hair tumbling over his eyes. The glass fell from his hand and splintered on the parquet flooring.

Slowly Mary rose, and watched his sprawling figure calmly, She opened her handbag and withdrew the dagger.

Thoughtfully, she closed her hand upon the cold haft. Her knuckles showed parchment white with the intensity of her grip.

Her mind went over all the ideas associated with Fred Tanner and Evelyn.

Evelyn had been her school friend, but in the last two years they had seen each other at infrequent intervals while Evelyn climbed the lower rungs of a glamorous, but uncertain stage career. Mary had known all about Evelyn's friendship with Tanner, who was a gambler, a hanger-on in society. No one knew how he contrived to make an income necessary to keep up his mode of living.

And now Evelyn was dead!

How she hated the suave Fred Tanner. Right from the start Mary had known he was unfit to lick Evelyn's shoes. Evelyn must have been mad to have associated with him. Evelyn who could surely have chosen from many men.

Mary had loved Evelyn in their schooldays, and there had always been a bond of affection between them whenever they met. Evelyn would give Mary a little present upon her birthday, and Mary would do the same when Evelyn's came round.

And now she was dead, and the man who had surely driven her to it lay drugged in his room, and the girl who hated him stood above him like an avenging angel, ready to strike.

Except for his regular breathing, the man lay still as a corpse. Mary slowly brought down the knife, but even as she did so, a feeling of revulsion swept over her. All at once Tanner's features seemed ugly and stupid. The veins of the neck stood out like little pipes. His breath came snoringly from between parted lips. Mary recoiled in horror. The whisky no longer braced her.

'Oh, God!' she cried. 'I want to get away. Let me get away!'

Tears started in her eyes, and a sudden surge of terror possessed her.

She darted to the door and then halted. What would happen if someone else should visit Tanner's flat after her and find him drugged? She would be blamed. Tanner might even take the matter to the police! He was calculating enough!

She went over to his sideboard desperately, wishing she could find something to revive the man. She searched aimlessly, not realising that it would be impossible to revive Tanner for some time, that the drug had done its work well.

How ironic it was! She had wanted the opportunity to kill him, and now that it was so clearly before her she felt only fear — a sickening blinding fear.

Among the miscellany of objects on the sideboard lay a letter — an open letter, in Tanner's handwriting. Automatically she read the first few words. Then she started. She picked up the letter, and began to read slowly, methodically. It was a love-letter.

'My darling Pam,
Everything will be arranged for the nineteenth, and we shall spend a glorious week before going on to Paris. I feel so intensely about you, I can hardly bear to linger in stuffy London for the next few days.

11

'Loving you as I do, what is there for you to fear? Your brother should leave you alone to manage your own life. You want to live thrillingly. A lovely girl should live — and love — and not submit to being buried in a country house where life is so slow.

'I love you, and together we shall be gloriously happy. Of this there can be no doubt.

'As to the ridiculous, practical details — leave everything to me. Perhaps it would be as well, however, if you do leave with as much money as you can possibly take. I think you should certainly bring along those Mexican Bonds you mention, and which are your share of your father's estate. They are yours by right, and I have a really remarkable opportunity to double their value for you in a matter of weeks, my dear.

'Well, hang all such prosaic details! I live in an atmosphere of delicious excitement, thinking of the time when you will come to me. To think that a mere few weeks ago you were unknown to me — you lovely creature! That this is Fate, I am positive. We were meant to find each other, and to live for each other only.

'And now I will leave all other topics until we meet and talk for hours in the old delightful way.

'Only one other thing before I close, my sweet. I do hope you will not speak to your brother. Honestly, darling, he does not understand you.

'And now I will break off in case I spoil the lovely things I have to tell you when we meet.'

The letter was signed: 'Your *humbly loving Fred.*'

Mary read the address on the newly written envelope, which lay beneath. 'Miss Pamela Shaw, The Laurels, Fernby.'

Mary had read without compunction. The utter hypocrisy of the remarkable script filled her with disgust. She could easily imagine the girl reading the boldly-written letter with a leaping heart.

Tanner's scheme was so obvious that Mary wondered how any girl could be

caught by such barefaced unscrupulous-
ness. Yet she could understand, in a way,
for Fred Tanner was an accomplished
conversationalist when he chose. He had
travelled — if one believed everything he
said so glibly — and his manners could
be those of a gentleman. He always had
money to spend, and he spent it with an
instinctive knowledge of the things dear
to the heart of a girl.

Yes, a pretty accomplished rogue was
Fred Tanner!

That Mary had distrusted him from the
start was simply instinctive dislike. Later
(and it was a remarkable example of
chance), she had learned from another
girl a great many things concerning him.
This girl was the daughter of wealthy
socialites, and she had entered Mary's hat
shop attracted by the beautiful models so
cleverly displayed, just as Fred Tanner
had been leaving with Evelyn Torrance on
his arm.

The newcomer, with a hostile stare at
the departing couple, coldly asked Mary
to show her some hats.

Ten minutes later she was very voluble

concerning Fred Tanner — very voluble in a surprisingly un-squeamish and nicely detailed way.

Afterwards, Mary had tried to tell Evelyn, but the rising young actress had simply laughed:

'My dear Mary, I hear the wildest rumours about everyone. Everyone is so insane. I can look after myself.'

Poor Evelyn! *'I can look after myself . . . '*

Mary stared at the letter again, and then at Fred Tanner's insensible body. If only the man were dead, then he could not spoil another young life . . .

But the fierce spark had gone from Mary. She felt limp, and close to exhaustion now that her emotions had run their extreme course. She wanted to get out.

She could see Tanner's game. He would spoil the girl called Pamela, take her money and anything she offered and then when he was tired of her, he would leave her. He would cast her aside probably in the worst circumstances.

Mary Calvin put the letter down again. Useless to destroy it, she felt. But she was going to stop Fred Tanner's rotten scheme: that she could at least do . . .

She would travel to Fernby and warn Pamela Shaw — and her brother — the brother of whom Fred Tanner seemed strangely afraid.

Mary opened the door of the flat and slipped out into the passage.

2

Mary is Rebuffed

Fred Tanner woke with a horrible feeling of numbness in his limbs and with a ghastly taste in his mouth. He drew himself from the armchair, stared round his flat in bewilderment. His eyes fell upon the electric clock and noted the time — 3 o'clock. Flashes of his talk with Mary Calvin sped through his brain. He shook his head as if to clear away confused images, and then stumbled over to the decanter on the sideboard, cursing his aching head and the things he could not explain.

After a drink he felt better, but still he could not understand why he had fallen asleep. He could not remember Mary Calvin leaving. Why the devil should he fall asleep?

He shook his head and wandered tiredly into the bedroom . . .

In the morning he felt his old self, but somewhat puzzled.

However, when he left the flat at ten-thirty he had thrust aside his unexplainable attack of sleepiness. He had other things to attend to.

* * *

He journeyed to Hammersmith and found a certain houseboat on the Thames. The boat lay moored to a grassy bank, lending an air of gaiety to the river. White paint and mahogany shone in the strong sun. Brass rails gleamed, testifying to someone's diligence. Tanner stepped aboard the clean deck-planks with a sardonic grin upon his smooth face.

He was at his sartorial best, in a finely-cut suit and silk shirt and tie. Perhaps it was a little out of place in a river setting, where flannels were the vogue, but Tanner had not journeyed to join a river-party.

He came to the cabin, knocked on the door, and entered immediately.

A bearded man was sitting on a stool,

admiring an unfinished canvas standing on an easel. He turned his head inquiringly, and when he saw Fred, the painter's eyes clouded angrily. He stood up, put to one side his brush and palette, wiped his hands on his smock and advanced towards Tanner.

'Hello, Merson,' said Tanner genially.

Merson Warren was a large man with fine white hands. Now those hands were clenched in anger and his dark, emotional eyes were stormy. He ran a hand through thick black hair, making it more than ever unruly.

Tanner placed his hat insolently upon an ornamental bronze bust and then sat down on a stool after carefully looking for paint spots. Merson Warren stood over him.

'You're here again!'

'Again,' acknowledged Fred. His thin lips sneered. Women found his smile charming until they looked back afterwards, and remembered with fear and rage . . .

'You want money?' questioned Merson Warren.

'Well, I didn't travel here to inquire about your health, Merson,' said Fred calmly. 'I want the usual fifty. Not much, but I understand you artist blokes are not lifting such great fees at the moment.'

'If things do not improve I shall be ruined,' said the other bitterly. 'And if you continue to blackmail me, I think I'll take my life. I'm tired, Tanner, tired and sick of it . . .'

The other frowned.

'Nonsense! You're a temperamental type; Merson. Life's sweet. You might even meet another Cynthia!'

Merson's eyes burned angrily.

'Sorry. I know you're touchy about Cynthia. Perhaps . . . ' Tanner paused. 'Perhaps that's why you murdered her. Anyway, here I am. You got rid of Cynthia in a sudden fit of jealousy, and dropped her into the Thames. You forgot to weight the sack, and she bobbed up. 'Murder!' said the police, but you could not be implicated. Now *I* could do more than implicate you, because I know the tramp who saw everything. And it cost me a few quid to keep that dirty little devil's mouth shut, Merson,' he ended plaintively.

'Do you have to repeat all that?' snapped Warren.

'No, I'll go immediately — if you've got fifty quid ready.'

Merson Warren's hands trembled. He hesitated, and then turned away with the bitterness of defeat within him.

He came back after having disappeared into the adjoining cabin, and found Fred coolly inspecting the unfinished canvas.

'Nice work! But where's the model?'

'She will soon be here,' The artist thrust a wad of notes at Tanner. 'Now go. And for heaven's sake leave me alone. I am a ghastly failure in life.'

'You sell your work?'

'I wish I could kill you!' said Merson hoarsely. 'That surely would be no great crime.'

For the second time in twenty-four hours Fred Tanner had heard those words. In his supreme self-confidence, he never attached much importance to threats, and even now he did not take Merson Warren's impulsive words seriously. He had entirely forgotten Mary

Calvin's utterance of the same threat. He laughed in Warren's face.

'You should infuse your passion into your work, my friend. I'll be seeing you again.'

He strolled out of the cabin, setting his hat at a jaunty angle as he stepped on to the deck.

Merson Warren watched his departure, anger etched deeply into his heavy features.

*   ★   *

At about the same time that Tanner was on Merson Warren's Thames houseboat, Mary Calvin went down to Fernby. She had left her hat shop in the competent charge of the abler of her two assistants, and journeyed by bus because she wanted to think, and the driving of her own car did not give her the chance. She was determined to smash Fred Tanner's scheme to get Pamela Shaw. It was one small way in which she could hit back on poor Evelyn Torrance's behalf.

She found The Laurels to be a smallish

country house of probably eight or nine rooms. It lay back from the road surrounded by the customary small park of shrubbery and trees. An iron gate swung loosely, and a gravel drive turned to the half hidden house. The building was a grey, old house, similar to hundreds up and down the country.

Mary stood outside the gate and looked for a sign of activity. But the house seemed to be slumbering in the midday summer sun.

She walked along the drive, a neat figure in a gay costume. Her long black pageboy hair was decorated by an absurdly chic hat poised at an engaging angle. Although she had set out in a deadly serious mood, she had a strong penchant for clothes and liked always to look attractive. She had taken to running a hat shop because millinery offered fair profit and she could not afford to ignore so excellent a source of income.

Her red shoes crunched the gravel as she determinedly approached the house. Then, within sight of the main door, she suddenly heard laughter. Away to the left a young girl was playing tennis with a tall young man, on what was evidently a private court. Instinctively. Mary guessed that she had found Pamela Shaw, and she walked purposefully towards the surround of the court.

The young man caught sight of Mary first. He glanced round, and stared for an appreciable time with what was obviously an admiring expression. Then he signalled to his partner, and turned to the door leading into the court.

He walked slowly to Mary, spinning his racket in his hand. She noticed his wrists were tanned and strong. A watch with a broad strap was fastened round his left wrist. He was fair, with his hair now a trifle ruffled.

'Were you . . . ?'

'I'm looking for Miss Pamela Shaw,' said Mary calmly.

'She'll be here in a second.' He was staring again, with what but for his pleasant expression, would have been unpardonable rudeness. She saw steady grey eyes, and knew instantly the owner had a passionate regard for truth and justice. He glanced back at his partner.

'My name's Alan Shaw,' he said.

'I'm Mary Calvin,' she told him frankly. 'Your sister has never met me before, but I would like to speak to her about a serious personal matter.'

He raised his eyebrows and smiled.

'For heaven's sake don't annoy Pam: She's been extremely nice these last three days — I'm wondering how much longer it will last.'

'I'll try not to annoy her,' said Mary in a low voice.

'I'm sure you wouldn't annoy anyone.'

And then Pamela Shaw ran up. With her first glance at the girl, Mary's heart sank a little, for she knew, as one woman will of another, that she was looking at a wilful, headstrong girl. Pamela could not be much older than twenty; and Mary with her twenty-four years felt suddenly mature. Pamela Shaw was pretty in a youthful, round-faced way. She had light brown hair like her brother, but whereas Alan had a jutting chin, the girl's chin was softly rounded.

Two eyes flicked over Mary.

25

'Hello,' Alan Shaw said: 'Pam, this is Mary Calvin. She would like to talk to you. I think I'll buzz off, if you'll excuse me.'

He slipped away tactfully. Left alone the two girls regarded each other for a long, silent moment.

'I might as well come straight to the point,' said Mary determinedly. 'I live in London, and once I had a friend called Evelyn Torrance. She killed herself, because of a man.'

'Then she was a fool,' said Pamela Shaw candidly. 'Go ahead, but I'm afraid I don't see the point.'

'The man's name was Fred Tanner,' Mary said. 'Now, please don't be annoyed. I know it isn't any affair of mine what you do, but I hope you will listen to me, I know Fred Tanner, and he is an utter beast. He has been mixed up with more women than is good for any man. Evelyn got into a horrible trouble through him, and she thought she was ruined, so she took her life.'

Pamela Shaw's lips had twisted rebelliously from the moment Mary spoke Tanner's name.

'Well, at least you've made the point clear now.' Pamela gripped her racket angrily. 'And I don't believe a word of it.'

'But it is true! Please let me tell you — '

'Fred has known a few girls, I'm quite aware. He has told me all about most of them.' Pamela's eyes snapped. 'And most of them were after his money.'

Mary gripped the other's arm. 'Don't be a fool! Fred Tanner has no money — at least not in the accepted sense. I have heard he makes money by gambling and in even less reputable ways.'

'You have heard!' repeated Pamela scornfully. 'Yes, you have heard, indeed. But why should I take your word for all this incredible nonsense about Fred? Let me tell you that he is the nicest man in the *world*! He has been amazingly good to me. Oh, I don't suppose I can make you understand. I think you are jealous. Fred is so good — that is why women spread such malicious rumours. I *hate* rumours!'

She was so young, so confident! Mary knew she had a fair measure of pigheadedness, too. Pamela was the type on whom reason and argument are lost, and obviously an argument with her could be an exasperating affair.

'You've wasted your time if you called to blacken Fred's character like this,' she snapped finally.

Mary drew a deep breath. She was glad she was no longer so impetuous as the other. Pamela was the sort of girl who would rush in where angels feared to tread, and land herself in a ghastly mess.

Mary felt she might batter reason into the other's head. Memories of Evelyn's lighthearted, *I can look after myself,* jabbed into her brain.

'I know that Tanner is sending you a letter arranging for you to run away with him. You are to spend a week somewhere, and then go on to Paris,' said Mary fiercely.

'How do you know that?' gasped Pamela.

'I read the letter in Fred Tanner's apartment last night,' retorted Mary. 'For heaven's sake, see reason. I don't want to see you ruined like Evelyn. Tanner asks you to bring money. I wonder how much your Mexican bonds are worth?'

The thrust made Pamela Shaw furious.

'I won't listen! I'd like to know what you, were doing in Fred's apartment! Perhaps you are one of the many disappointed!'

'I went along to kill him,' said Mary, evenly.

'You're mad!' Pamela raised her arm in her fury, but let it drop without striking the intended blow. 'Get out of these grounds. I don't believe a word you say.'

And she walked quickly away, swinging her racket furiously.

Mary moved slowly. She found Alan Shaw standing at the bend in the drive. He looked at her quizzically.

Mary went straight up to him.

'You've got to stop your sister from making a horrible fool of herself,' she said.

'I can see you've been having the dickens of a row,' he said. 'Come over to the summerhouse. Tell me all about it.'

3

Other Activities

At the moment Fred Tanner felt that life was highly enjoyable. He had posted a letter to the girl he intended to fool around with for a few weeks — perhaps months. Who knew? Everything would run like clockwork; of that he felt sure. For Tanner was one of those incredible men who lead lives of luxury and ease and are impelled to batten on the follies of credulous women. Life to him was a sort of jungle, and every pretty face that of a potential victim. If she had money, so much the better. If not, then some extraordinary adventure, pandering to his immense conceit, would be quickly and viciously engineered.

Lies, deceit and astonishing masquerades were Tanner's stock in trade. He had worn the uniforms of every service and rank, and had patronised various exclusive clubs until the whispers about him grew in volume and his past rose up against him. Then he would gather in his gains and vanish, to the bewilderment of those who claimed his acquaintance.

Tanner was a Londoner born and bred, and it was his policy to live fairly quietly in London — he had no desire to quit the city. He confined most of his adventures to the big towns of the provinces, only now and again lying his way into some web of deceit inside the capital.

He had returned to the City after leaving Merson Warren's studio houseboat, the fifty pounds nestling comfortably inside his notecase. Approaching a gaunt, dingy apartment house in the King's Cross area, he entered and climbed the stairs to a top-floor room. The man who let him in walked to a table and sat down. He was in his shirtsleeves, and a cigarette dangled from his lips. His mouth was creased with lines giving him an expression of chronic moroseness.

'Look, Tanner, you're on to something easy now,' he said, opening a steel deed box, and pulling out two wads of money.

'Easy money, I say. I've had some rotten times before I got good jobs like this. Here, look at them! Currency notes — *and* as clever as you like.'

Fred Tanner slipped the rubber band off one wad and selected a note, which he held to the light.

'They seem good,' he admitted.

'You can have as many as you like,' said the other. 'Dirt cheap, too. The Big Boy says he'll let them go at fifty for twenty-five quid real money.'

'You can give me a hundred,' rejoined Tanner. 'That's enough for the moment. It will take a few days to get rid of a hundred in dud notes. Here is your fifty quid.'

Tanner brought out his wallet and Merson Warren's fifty pounds paid for the spurious money. Then he laughed.

'The Big Boy undoubtedly has an excellent method of distributing his fake notes. Getting rid of forged money is confoundedly dangerous. Anyone can print the stuff.'

'Not like the Boy,' observed Ted Leesing, shaking his head. 'This splosh is perfect. You take no risk, Mister Tanner.'

'The Boy takes no risks you mean,' said Tanner unpleasantly.

'Take it or leave it,' said Leesing, unruffled. 'There are plenty of buyers,'

'I'm taking the stuff because I think I can soon turn it over,' retorted Tanner.

He stowed the notes away carefully, then went down the dirty stairs, whistling softly.

As he reached the pavement and strolled along, a face momentarily appeared at the top floor window. Could Tanner have seen the sneering expression of hatred as the man stared down, he might have felt a twinge of apprehension. But Ted Leesing's face disappeared, and the grimy windows again gazed blankly across the street to other grimy windows.

Tanner spent the afternoon exchanging counterfeit notes. His practice was to enter a hotel bar, order a whisky and pay with a fake note, buy a second drink, and leave casually.

In this manner he spent a pleasant afternoon. His act became more polished with every performance, until after seven or eight bars had been visited and a number of whiskies had been consumed, the danger of his visiting a hotel twice in the same two hours became quite real.

He went home by taxi, rearranging his wallet during the journey, and when paying the driver discovered to his surprise that it contained nothing but notes ... The taxi driver managed to effect the change, Tanner bestowing a large tip.

As the driver pulled away, he walked the two remaining blocks to his flat. His drinking had not muddled him so that he desired a return visit from the taxi-driver. If the driver now discovered he had been caught with a dud note, he would have difficulty in tracing his cagey client.

He ate a meagre lunch in the service restaurant of his block of flats, and then feeling drowsy went to his rooms. He tore off his jacket and shoes and stretched himself on his bed. He was soon fast asleep.

He slept well, and it was nearly seven when he awoke. He felt cold, irritable. He walked slowly info his bathroom, proceeded with a lengthy toilet — his vanity extended to his personal appearance. He shaved, rubbed an eau-de-Cologne tonic into his hair, and dressed meticulously in evening clothes. He had decided to visit a smart West-End nightclub where he was well-known, and, what was most important, favourably regarded.

He was dressed and tasting his first whisky of the evening, when his bell rang crisply.

He walked to the door, hesitated a moment and then opened it.

'Hello, Fred, darling!'

A girl slipped into the room. She smiled with bold grey eyes.

'Pamela! My dear girl, this is a surprise! I have just posted a letter to you today!'

Fred Tanner caught her hands. Though indeed surprised, he went smoothly into his act. He was the perfect lover, adoring a girl who thrilled him. He was heartily glad that he was looking his best, and this very fact filled him with a pleasant emotion. He began to feel that he was really in love with this young girl.

'I had to talk with you, Fred.'

He led her to a settee, and switched on

an electric fire. Within a few seconds the simply-furnished flat seemed very cosy, and an admirable place for confidences.

He kissed her masterfully. He knew that when a woman is in any sort of trouble a convincing display of masculinity is the very thing.

'Fire away, Pam. Heavens, how desirable you are!'

She looked into his brown eyes, saw nothing but passionate regard there, and all her doubts fell away.

'Well, I was visited today at Fernby by a woman who called herself Mary Calvin. She tried to poison my mind against you, Fred. She said the most dreadful things . . .'

He did not show his surprise that Mary Calvin should know anything about Pamela Shaw. Instead he bit his lip, and made all the pretence of controlled annoyance, but at the same time his brain was working furiously.

'So Mary Calvin called upon you,' he said at last, in a subdued tone. 'She is a most annoying person. I cannot say less than that. If I told you everything . . .'

He broke off. His right hand fingers tattooed impatiently upon his knee.

'I wish you would tell me something about her,' breathed Pamela. 'Honestly, she talked on and on — such terrible things, Fred.'

'I can easily imagine her words,' said Fred heavily. His arm tightened round her waist, as if to suggest that they could never be separated by the futility of words. 'Mary Calvin is just another girl whose character is not so innocent as her face. She worked with me in a theatrical venture — I think I've told you about it before — and like some others, she assumed an awful lot simply because I tried to help her. She has some talent as an actress — you probably received an example of it — and I tried to develop her. Like the others, she is too emotional. These women! Their emotional minds could distort the universe! They talk about me, lie about me, my life is sometimes a nightmare because of them!'

His fingers bit into her arms as if from the fierceness of his feelings.

'You believe me, Pamela?' he cried.

'I do Fred!' She turned her pretty face upwards. Her lips were parted, her eyes glowing. Fred Tanner drew her slowly to him and kissed her passionately.

'But my darling, you should really shake these fools off,' said Pamela at last. 'This Mary Calvin told me all about our — our — arrangements for the nineteenth. She said that she read a letter here, in your flat, and that she had tried to kill you!'

He laughed at the concern in her young eyes. All the same, his ready wits accepted this explanation as to how Mary Calvin had come to learn of Pamela.

'We shall shake her off — when we leave town before the Paris trip, dearest.'

'How did Mary Calvin come to read your letter?' asked Pamela earnestly.

Tanner said in a low voice: 'She came here the other night and was about to make a scene. I had just finished writing to you. She grabbed the letter and read most of it before I succeeded in taking it from her. She was a little violent, and I hated to struggle with her, but it had to be done.'

She snuggled against him, content now that her doubts were set at ease.

Tanner smiled to himself. His mind raced over the points of his story. He had covered himself well.

Undoubtedly Pamela Shaw was a young fool, but Tanner well knew that infatuation could blind almost anyone.

'Darling, are you returning to Fernby tonight?' he asked

'I think I will. But I had to see you.'

'I understand perfectly,' he said softly. 'But before you return, let's pop out to some place. I know a little restaurant in Soho where we can dine. But I'll change. A suit is more appropriate for Lugi's place.'

'Thank goodness we aren't going to be too swell,' laughed Pamela. She looked down at her well-cut costume, smoothed it with her hands. 'I simply rushed away from Fernby leaving Alan talking to the Calvin woman. Their pow-wow had lasted quite a few hours, for he had invited her to stay for lunch. Discussing me, I think; so I left.'

'What does it matter?' Tanner gestured

with a snap of his fingers. 'On the nineteenth we go away together. Two more days, Pam,' he said breathlessly.

Once more she was in his arms, and he held her with all the actor's assured technique.

'I'll have settled the bookings and other arrangements by the nineteenth,' he said. 'I have been pretty thorough in my study of the Mexican Bonds. I want to get tip-top prices for your holdings, Pam, my sweet.'

And the sophisticated Pamela Shaw smiled up to him, completely under his spell.

Tanner returned in a few minutes, when they went down by lift to the street. A cab rank lay at the end of the block. Tanner set off to traverse the hundred yards, guiding the girl. The street was empty of people and quietly illuminated. Suddenly a taxi ran smoothly down the street and pulled-in alongside Tanner and the girl.

'Taxi, sir?' called the driver.

Tanner laughed, and tipped his hat to the back of his head. He threw away his cigarette and exhaled smoke. He guided Pamela to the now stationary taxi.

'To Lugi's in Snell Street,' he told the driver.

As they climbed in, the driver nodded, his big peaked cap moving up and down above the large upturned collar.

The car drove off with a surge of power. Tanner lay back, reaching for his cigarette case, and smiled at Pamela.

Suddenly the driver began to sing softly. Tanner's hand was arrested in the act of extracting a cigarette.

'Lovely lady,
I'm falling madly,
In love with you!'

Cursing involuntarily upon hearing the softly-sung words, his cigarette case slipped back into his pocket, he reached a hand out to the door handle.

The driver took both hands from the wheel and for a second fumbled with something apparently slung round his neck.

Then he braked hard and stopped the

car. He turned to stare at the rear seat.

Pamela gave a gasp at the man's appearance. Tanner's brain grasped the significance of the respirator clamped over the man's nose and mouth.

Raising a syringe-like object the taxi-man pressed the plunger. Within seconds the air was filled with sickly sweet fumes. Tanner choked, wrenched at the door handle but the driver was too quick for him and, in addition those sweet, paralysing fumes were clouding his senses with incredible rapidity. Tanner's hand was knocked from the door handle. As Pamela leaned forward, she was pushed roughly back to the cushions.

Tanner made one last effort to raise himself from his seat.

But his muscles seemed turned to lifeless pulp. He fell back, down, down, down ... At his side Pamela stretched herself uneasily, with a little cry. Her eyes closed, she gasped, and then began to breathe slowly, rhythmically like a deep-sleeper.

Within sixty seconds the two occupants of the taxi were quite unconscious. The man with the respirator watched them closely, and then swung back to the wheel, starting the car, and setting off with swift acceleration down the road.

4

The Trunk

Mary Calvin pressed the bell of Fred Tanner's flat. Inside the apartment, she could hear the soft ring of the bell but no other sound came to her ears. She turned to Alan Shaw.

'He must be out.'

Alan made no comment. He glanced quickly up and down the deserted passage, and then brought a bunch of keys from his pocket. He fitted one into the lock. A few tentative twists and then the door swung open an inch. Alan Shaw withdrew the key and slipped the bunch into his pocket.

'One of the peculiar advantages of having been an Intelligence Officer in His Majesty's service is that one sometimes obtains these useful implements known commonly as skeleton keys,' he said calmly, and smiled.

They slipped into Tanner's flat, and Alan gently closed the door behind them.

'I hope the porter does not pop in,' he murmured.

Mary found herself liking the man. For all his quips she knew he was greatly worried about Pamela, and the manner in which she had dashed from The Laurels. Mary had suggested that Pamela might run to Fred Tanner. Alan Shaw had listened to her story, and to her relief had believed her. From him she discovered that Pamela had been running in wild company while he had been away on a confidential mission. Their parents were dead, and The Laurels was looked after by an elderly housekeeper and staff. Pamela had wanted to leave, taking her share of her father's money, and live in a London flat, but Alan was her guardian and trustee of her money until she was twenty-one. That was not for another year, and Alan had quashed the scheme by withholding funds.

'What happens now that we have broken in?' asked Alan.

'We could wait until Tanner returns,'

45

said Mary. She added hopefully: 'Then you could give him the hiding of his life, and take Pamela home. I'd enjoy the fight.'

He smiled.

'So would I, but I don't care much for waiting. I wonder if Pamela really called here? The awful little fool!'

'Why not search the flat for anything Tanner might consider his special secrets?' asked Mary calmly.

'You hate him, I can see, my girl,' said Alan wryly.

He went over to a writing desk. The drawers were locked, and the leather-laid top was bare. He fished out his bunch of keys again, and opened the drawers methodically. Most of the contents were of little or no interest. But one drawer produced an odd assortment of newspaper cuttings and notebooks, which Alan studied with some care. Mary came to his side and looked over his arm. Some of the cuttings referred to a mysterious figure who had carried out several confidence tricks some months before. Other cuttings were about a number of big-scale frauds, and details of imposters who had received stiff prison sentences. Although Alan guessed that the 'mystery figure' might well be Tanner and that he kept the cuttings to satisfy his vanity, he could not understand why he should interest himself in escapades which had been no immediate concern of his and whose instigators were now in jail.

Among the general litter there was also a notebook containing a few addresses and to some of these were pencilled notes and names and the references suggested that Tanner had his fingers in a number of dubious activities of fairly wide range.

But Fred Tanner kept most of his confidences locked within his brain, and Mary's 'special secret' did not materialise.

Alan closed the drawers. He turned to Mary and stood with his hands in his pockets.

'Perhaps it would be better if we went outside and waited. I'm not fond of waiting at any time, but perhaps it has its virtues.'

'Surely Intelligence Officers have their share of patience?'

'Well — yes — red tape is rather trying to one's patience. Still, in the circumstances, I think we'd better get out of here.'

Mary laughed.

'Yes, we want to find Pam and not be taken in charge to the nearest police station.

They left Tanner's flat, and walked out calmly through the lobby. Alan nodded to the night porter. Outside, in the cool night air, they paused.

'We'll find a restaurant and wait . . . ' began Alan, when a car drew up at the curb, and two police officers climbed out. They were large, deliberate men. They closed the door of the patrol car, and crossed the pavement unhurriedly. Their faces were set and grim.

Alan watched them curiously, halting Mary. The two policemen walked straight into the main entrance of the block of flats the couple had just left. When they had disappeared, Alan sauntered back to the lobby with Mary. They paused, hearing quite distinctly one of the policemen ask to be shown to Tanner's flat.

Alan smiled and drew Mary aside.

'It seems our friend is in trouble with his more natural enemies. I wonder why they want to interview Tanner? Like us, they'll be unlucky.'

Some ten minutes later the policemen reappeared. Alan intercepted them on their way back to the patrol car.

'I should like to find Mr. Fred Tanner, too,' he remarked, pointedly.

He received a careful scrutiny.

'Why should you want to see him?'

'I think he is planning to run off with my sister, and I am determined to stop him.'

One of the policemen, a sergeant, said: 'We should like to question Mr. Tanner, too, sir,' He surveyed Alan quietly weighing up his man. He seemed to reach a decision. 'We have received information from an anonymous source,' he said, 'that Tanner is in possession of counterfeit money.'

Alan whistled. 'Another of friend Tanner's pleasant pastimes!'

'Well, it is not proven,' said the sergeant cautiously. 'We get all sorts of queer messages, and they are often a pack of lies. Still, we've got to make inquiries. Have you any idea where Mr. Tanner might be, sir?'

'Not the slightest, otherwise I'd be away after him.'

'Well, we'll be returning to question Mr. Tanner later,' declared the police officer. 'If you have a charge to make, please come along to headquarters.'

'I don't want publicity,' said Alan slowly. 'I might be able to make Tanner change his mind myself.'

The sergeant smiled, and with his companion he turned to the patrol car.

When the car had drawn away, Alan said: 'So the police are after Fred Tanner, too. It seems to me that Mr. Tanner is in for a hot time, one way or the other.'

He was walking slowly, thoughtfully, his hand on Mary's arm. Then, as the sound of a car braking came to his ears, he turned swiftly, and looked back.

A shabby van had pulled up at the entrance to the flats. Alan saw the driver hop out and go round to the back of it. Alan stood, staring interestedly. Mary glanced at him.

With the doors of the van wide open, the driver bawled across the pavement to the porter who had appeared leisurely.

'Hi, mate! Like to give me a 'and with this blinking box? For Mr. Tanner, it is. Heavy, I can tell yer.'

The night porter approached reluctantly.

Alan Shaw applied a gentle pressure to Mary's arm. They strolled back a few yards and Alan calmly watched as the van driver and porter struggled with a large chest.

The two men set their burden on the pavement.

'Hell, it's blinking 'eavy!' gasped the van driver. 'Wonder what 'e's got in 'ere — a chunk of machinery?'

'How did you get it on your van?' asked the night porter, more for the sake of prolonging the rest than to satisfy his curiosity.

'Well, the bloke helped me on with it. I'd been waiting long enough for 'im to come out with the chest. My van had been ordered, see? Just this afternoon a bloke phoned my 'ouse and asked me to do a moving job for 'im. I had to bring the van down to No. 2, Ritson's Lane, over towards Waterloo, a cramped-looking place. So I brings it down, and 'as to wait a bit. Then the bloke drags the chest out. We hauls it on the van, and I'm a bit fed up with waiting, see? So I jumps into my seat and pulls out of the lane without any more palaver. I'd got my thirty bob before the chest got in my van, you bet, and I knew my address. So here I am, mate.'

The van driver concluded his story with a snort. The porter, having recovered his breath, stooped to the chest and, with a jerk of his head, indicated that the driver should do the same.

'Let me help you,' said Alan Shaw.

'It's all right, sir,' muttered the porter, but he made no actual effort to prevent Alan's helping him. Alan gripped the chest, and they went slowly into the lobby towards the lift.

Mary followed cautiously, but for some strange reason she felt an unaccountable upsurge of fear within her. She shivered and drew together the lapels of her coat.

The porter had a master key to

Tanner's flat, and opening the door, he switched on the light. The heavy chest was dumped down in a conveniently bare space. The van driver stared round.

'Mr. Tanner not at home?'

The porter shook his head. The van driver looked disgruntled, realising his hope of a tip from Mr. Tanner had faded. The men stood for a moment in a small, silent group. And then Alan slowly opened his hands, palms upwards, and stared at the sticky red stain daubing his fingers.

'Open that case,' he said authoritatively. 'This is blood.'

Mary, standing in the doorway, drew in her breath sharply.

'Blood?' said the van driver incredulously.

But Alan was examining the locks on the chest. They were fairly heavy brass clasps, and the chest was made of strong leather and fibre, though now in rather a dilapidated condition.

Alan tried his skeleton key, only to discover that the old case would not yield. He picked up a heavy brass dog, which ornamented the fireplace, and hammered at the clasps forcing them from their sockets. Under this treatment one part of the left hand lock came away altogether, and the other sprang open.

Alan raised the lid, after a warning glance to Mary to stay beside the door.

The body of a man lay curled in grotesque and hideous fashion in the trunk. A great clot of blood had formed on the breast of his coat and a thin red streak extended from his nostril to the comer of his mouth.

'This is not Tanner,' said Alan slowly.

'Hell, ruddy murder!' exclaimed the startled driver.

The old night porter paled. 'Who is it, sir?'

'I don't know,' said Alan. He jerked his eyes to Mary.

'Phone the police, Mary,' he said crisply.

The body was that of a large bearded man, with thick black hair. Looking at the nondescript suit in which the body was attired, Alan noticed spots of various coloured paints on the fabric. He picked up the man's wrist, felt for the pulse.

To his astonishment, he noticed a feeble movement.

'Get this man out of the chest,' he snapped. 'He's not dead. Quick, now!'

The three men laid their burden on a settee. Alan found some of Tanner's whisky, and administered a dose at once.

Mary Calvin appeared in the doorway.

'I phoned from a telephone in the hall,' she said. 'The police will soon be over.' Her eyes fell in fascinated horror to the body on the settee. Alan noticed the glance and said:

'Better phone again, Mary. Tell them an ambulance is needed. This man might live if he is rushed to hospital.'

Mary turned, glad to leave the ghastly sight, and as if to prove Alan's words true, the dying man opened his eyes. In full vigour they were fine eyes. Now the haze of oncoming death seemed to fog them. Alan gave him more whisky.

The spirit seemed to revive the man's ebbing strength. Alan witnessed an astonishing, if temporary revival of the man's life-urge. Words came slowly from the dying man's lips. Whether he knew there were friends beside him or not, he seemed possessed by a desperate determination to speak. He raised his head with an effort so dreadful that his very eyes seemed to start from their sockets.

'Tanner . . . Tanner . . . Tanner . . . ' He repeated the name as if it were the clue to everything.

'Tanner . . . shot . . . me . . . '

And then the head fell back. Alan jerked glances at the other two men.

'Better remember all this,' he said. 'The police might require you as witnesses.'

Alan gave the man yet another sip of whisky. It was obvious to him that the poor devil had not much longer to live. The ambulance, so optimistically called for, would take away a corpse.

Again after the sip of whisky the man revived, though this time slowly and uncertainly. His eyelids opened as if lead weights dragged on them.

Alan whispered: 'Who are you?'

The answer was barely audible. 'Merson . . . Warren . . . ' The man slipped again into oblivion. For a full minute Alan thought they had seen the end. Then, as if energy had been gathered for a final surge, the man's dying whisper came again. 'Tanner . . . is taking . . . the girl . . . houseboat . . . Hammersmith.'

Life was slipping from Merson Warren's large frame. There was little Alan or anyone else could do.

The tense group in the room caught distant sounds of approaching men. A lift whined and stopped. Footsteps were heard in the passage. Mary had returned in time to hear the man's last words. Now she opened the door of the room as the footsteps approached, and admitted the police.

An inspector from the C.I.D. led the way, followed by two uniformed policemen.

'I'm Detective-Inspector Lumley,' he barked. 'I'll need statements from you all.'

'This poor devil is not yet dead,' said Alan. 'Where — ?'

'The ambulance will be here any second,' interrupted the man from the C.I.D., 'with a doctor.'

To Mary Calvin the next thirty seconds

were a confused period in which the ambulance men appeared and a doctor announced that Merson Warren was dead. Then for fully half-an-hour there were shrewd questions put to her and the others, while photographs of the body and the chest were taken. Then, while the van driver was still undergoing interrogation, the body was taken away in the ambulance to the police mortuary.

It was fully an hour later when Alan and Mary found themselves outside Tanner's flat, and they could talk freely.

Alan had told the police about Tanner's plan to run away with his sister. The van-driver and the porter had verified Merson Warren's last statement about Tanner's intention to take a girl to a houseboat at Hammersmith.

'No doubt the police will go down to Hammersmith immediately,' said Alan. 'And perhaps they'll visit Ritson's Lane, too. We can only visit one place at a time, so I think we'll take a taxi and try to find this houseboat. The girl Tanner is taking there must be Pamela.'

'Why should Tanner send the body of a

dying man back to his own flat?' asked Mary, determinedly seizing on the point that had puzzled them all.

Alan uttered a curt laugh.

'Why, indeed? Why should he murder the man? And have it planned in advance, if the van driver's testimony is correct?'

They came to the nearby taxi rank, and Alan swiftly gave instructions to a cabby.

'I want to find a houseboat on the Thames in the Hammersmith area. I don't know the name of the houseboat or anything much about it, but I want you to get me to the river first, and we'll take it up from there.'

The driver did not argue. Within seconds the taxi moved swiftly away. Alan leaned back against the cushions.

'Mary, if we find Tanner before the police I'd like to get Pamela away quickly. I'd hate to think of her making headlines with this swine if the police capture him.'

'I hope the police do get Tanner. This might be the end of his terrible career, but still,' replied Mary excitedly, 'I'm dreadfully anxious to help your sister.'

'Perhaps I should send you back home,'

said Alan reflectively. 'Tanner might be dangerous — if we catch up with him.'

'I'm not going home,' said Mary definitely.

His hand caught hers for a moment. The slight contact sent a thrill through Mary's heart. Then she quickly withdrew her hand.

'Finding Tanner might be like looking for the proverbial needle in a haystack,' said Alan thoughtfully.

The taxi made smooth unbroken progress while Alan and Mary each smoked a cigarette. Then the taxi driver braked and halted. He pushed aside a sliding glass partition and spoke to Alan.

'Here, sir. We're near the river. I think there are a few 'ouseboats in the next half-mile.'

Alan climbed out into the twilight, and stood staring at the dull sheen of water lying at the foot of the riverbank.

The road curved abruptly from the grassy bank, but a track led parallel with the river. A hundred yards away Alan could see the darker bulk of a row of houses, their lawns stretching down to the river. He thought he could see the lights of a houseboat at the riverside.

All at once the slenderness of his chance of meeting Tanner struck him. The dying man could easily be mistaken. Tanner might not take a girl to a houseboat on the Thames. He might change his mind. He might have other plans. Anyway why should he choose a houseboat?

Then his thoughts were broken by the approaching whine of a powerful engine. Alan watched as a big saloon car tore up the road, taking the curve from the river with effortless speed. Alan noticed the rod-like radio attachment.

'The police car,' he muttered. 'Well, they aren't stopping at this part of the river.'

Alan turned to the cab again.

'I would like you to wait for us, driver. Don't worry, we aren't bilks — I'll pay for the outward journey now. Don't be surprised if we are gone some time. I'll square with you later,'

He paid the driver handsomely, and the man settled back in his seat, gratified.

Alan helped Mary to alight.

'The police car has just passed,' said Alan. 'Perhaps they are going to try visiting the houseboats lower down. Well, we've got just as much chance to find Tanner as they have. They seem to be a little slow in getting off the mark, though they are always sure.'

He gripped Mary's arm. They walked along the riverbank. The sky was darkening and a few stars were becoming visible.

'Tanner will have the police after him until he is captured,' observed Mary.

'I have no objection to that,' said Alan. 'But I should like to find Pamela before the police get her for interrogation. That is the rotten part. She has done nothing wrong, but some confounded reporter will surely pick on her as the feminine angle. You know the stuff; 'Killer Hides With Girl in Houseboat'. And if Tanner gets away,' he continued grimly, 'he'll probably take Pamela with him. That is supposing she knows nothing about the murder of Merson Warren. I can hardly imagine Pam sticking to Tanner if she knew he was a murderer.'

'It's almost certain Pamela ran away from Fernby to see Tanner,' observed Mary, 'And that means they've been together all this evening, yet Tanner has committed a murder. I don't understand it, I just don't.' She frowned in perplexity.

Alan peered along the path as it twisted through tall bushes.

'There's our first houseboat, moored by that grass bank,' he said. 'Let's start inquiries.'

Even as he urged Mary along by his side; two dark figures plunged wildly along the path towards them. It seemed they had fought their way desperately through the bushes to reach the path.

Alan's big form blocked the way, Mary was slightly behind him, startled by the madly scrambling figures.

And then, in a matter of seconds, the two parties met, unavoidably, and Alan's arms went round the man, halting him. A girl stood behind, panting.

'You fool!' hissed Tanner. 'You fool, Shaw! The police are after us. Keep moving!'

Tanner had instantly recognised Pamela's brother. He knew, too, that Mary

Calvin was standing behind Alan. Tanner exerted his strength to escape Alan's grip, but failed to even shake his opponent.

Alan looked past Tanner to Pamela's face, now hidden in shadows. Her laboured breathing made him tighten his lips.

'Pam, I'm taking you away from this man. Let the police have him. He's a murderer!'

Tanner snarled his reply:

'You fool, Shaw! You had better not waste another second. I don't understand how you or the police learnt so soon that Warren is dead, but the fact is Pamela shot Merson Warren!'

Alan struck Tanner once across the face, a backhanded blow.

'Tell your lies to the police!'

And then Pamela's anguished wail:

'But it's true, Alan! It's true!'

5

The Truth About Merson Warren

Alan Shaw was not stampeded by Pamela's cry, but he knew instinctively that his course of action must now be to avoid the police. He grasped that fact in exactly one second.

One thing he knew — he must have time in which to sort things out and see how his sister could be protected. He wanted to get to the core of truth in Pamela's cry.

He pushed Tanner ahead. The man tried to jerk free as Alan thrust him along the path, but Alan seized the other's arm savagely, bending it upwards and backwards. Once Tanner struck out with his free arm, but Alan dodged the wild blow. Then Tanner suddenly realised his efforts were hindering his escape from the police, if not his freedom from his captor. He went along in sullen silence.

Alan called in a low, urgent voice to Mary:

'Bring Pam along! To the taxi. Hurry!'

In truth Mary had little need to press the other girl along. Pamela Shaw was gasping as they ran, and Mary sensed this was because of deep fear as much as exhaustion. Mary's mind was reeling from the sense of Pamela's desperate words. It didn't seem credible! Why should Pamela kill Merson Warren? Hadn't Tanner placed the body in the chest and helped hoist it on to the van?

There again the incredible fact mocked at her. Why should Tanner send a dying man, crammed horribly into a box, to his own flat?

Mary tried to dispel these fruitless questions from her mind. Alan had ordered them to run for the taxi, that, now, was the one important objective.

Alan thrust Tanner ahead at full speed, with an occasional backward glance to see that Pamela and Mary were following. He ran lightly as an athlete, hurrying with sureness along the uneven riverbank. Tanner often stumbled, and Alan jerked him up, taking the sudden strain deftly. Tanner cursed. When they finally saw the road, higher up the riverbank, he said:

'Better watch for the cops, Shaw. You wouldn't like your sister to be brought up before the magistrates in the morning!' And then he continued, as if the thought had just occurred to him, 'The police are quick but, thank heavens, they dash around in those unmistakable cars of theirs! I saw one against the sky as it tore along the high road. I was on the deck, and the road runs high above the river there. It made a perfect silhouette. Spotted it straight away!' A strange note of pride crept into his voice. 'I knew they were after me — and your sister — so we ran. They could hardly be down here for nothing, I guessed.'

They climbed the bank to the road, cautiously but rapidly. The taxi was there, with the driver sitting at his wheel. Alan strode forward and opened the taxi door, bundling Tanner inside.

The driver sat up at this sudden reappearance of his fares. Alan hurried Mary and Pamela into the rear compartment of the car. The he rapped on the glass panel and said:

'Take us back into the city — towards Paddington Station.'

The taxi moved forward and sped swiftly down the road.

'Before we get to the station, you're going to tell me the truth of everything that has happened.' Alan sat beside Tanner on the tilt-seat. He still held his arm, and he ran his hand over his clothes, seeking for the gun the other might have. 'Now, how is it possible to say Pamela killed Merson Warren?'

'It's quite a story,' drawled Tanner. His composure was complete again. 'But you can be sure Pam shot him.'

'I'm not at all sure. I want to know the truth.'

Pamela broke in

'Alan — it is horribly true. But it was self-defence. The man had kidnapped us.'

Alan looked across to his sister. He guessed that Pamela's strong, wilful self-confidence had received a shattering blow. She was holding her two hands to her head, the palms flat against her temples as if to still a throbbing nerve. There was little Mary could do except hold her shoulders.

'Perhaps you can tell me the story better than Tanner,' suggested Alan quietly.

'I'll try, but — but — it is all so crazy, Alan. I left home and came to Fred's flat to see him and talk. I wanted to talk oh, so badly, I felt I *must* talk to him! Later we went out and got into a taxi. The car had hardly moved away when the driver began to sing some idiotic song, and then he turned round and pumped some awful drug at us!' She paused, and then went on;

'Oh, Alan, when I came to again I was lying in a ghastly dark cellar, and the taxi driver had removed his cap and respirator. Then Fred regained consciousness. The man, whose name turned out to be Merson Warren, began taunting us. He was going to kill us. He had intended to kill Fred because he said he was blackmailing him. I think he must have been mad for he called Fred some filthy names.'

'I can imagine that,' commented Alan. 'Go on, Pam.'

'Warren said he did not really want to kill me, but he had hoped to get Fred alone. Now that I knew his identity, he would have to kill us both. He rambled on, waving a gun and uttering mad threats. He said he had arranged to have Fred's body taken to a safe place. A man was calling with a van, expecting to take away an old chest.'

Pamela swallowed, brought her hands down on her lap and locked them tightly together.

'He said that the van man would take Fred's dead body away. Warren looked at his watch, and muttered something about it being nearly time. Then he said I would have to die. He said I would be left in the cellar because the chest was not big enough for two. Oh, it was ghastly, Alan. Warren seemed to see some horrid joke when he spoke of Fred's body going to a safe place in the old chest. He laughed and pushed Fred with his foot.'

'Then very suddenly Fred jumped up and I thought Warren was ready to shoot him. I shrieked and rose, too. It was all very confusing. But Warren was amazingly slow. He fumbled as if his crazy mind had taken away all sense of reality causing him to think we couldn't strike back. The gun dropped from his hand. Fred struggled with him for some time — perhaps it was merely seconds, but I watched horrified. Then Fred stumbled. Warren pushed him away. I saw the opportunity to dive for the gun. The next moment I was holding it, pointing the gun at the man. I had never held a gun in my life. I wasn't sure that I was even holding it properly, but I tried to bluff. I felt desperately grim. Then — then I shot Warren.'

Pamela's voice choked. She began to speak again through clenched teeth.

'I'll tell you the truth, Alan. Fred and I both shot Warren.'

'Both?' Her brother snapped the interrogation.

'Yes. As I was holding the gun, Fred turned round to me. He drew me aside and placed his hand over my hand hold-ing the gun, and the next instant there was a deafening noise. Warren fell at once.'

'Tell us the rest, Pam,' said Alan grimly, and his grip on Tanner tightened.

'Well,' Fred shouted out, 'That's yours, Warren, you devil!' His face looked awful — white and drawn. He stood in thought for a moment — and then he picked up Warren's body and began to — to pack him into the chest — Oh, it was horrible!' Pamela began to weep with heart-tearing sobs. The taxi sped along the road. No one spoke for a time. Then Pamela dried her eyes, and began to talk again.

'I could hardly watch while the man was placed in the chest. I thought he was dead, and so did Fred, even though he had shouted at him. Then there was a knock and a man's voice outside saying he had called for the load. It was the man with the van. Fred snapped down the catches on the chest, and dragged it outside into the lane while I stayed hidden. Oh, my thoughts, Alan! In that dark cellar it was a living nightmare! Fred returned a few minutes later, and we heard the van drive off. He then said, 'Let's get over to Warren's houseboat. God knows what papers the swine may have left to blackguard me!'

'But,' said Alan grimly, 'Tanner actually fired that shot?'

Tanner laughed sneeringly.

'Oh, so you're trying to place the blame on me? Don't be so hopeful. We *both* shot Warren.'

'In a court it would undoubtedly be ruled as self-defence,' snapped Alan.

'Perhaps, but I don't want it taken to court, if I can help it. Too many other things might come out.'

'Fred!' Pamela's despairing cry fluttered across the compartment. She stared at him. Mary sensed that the girl was seeing the blackguardly side of Tanner for the first time.

'Of course, you didn't realise that the van driver had been ordered to take that old chest to your flat,' commented Alan, quietly, 'Apparently this was Warren's idea of a grim joke — to send your body back to your own flat in a trunk.'

Alan felt Tanner start violently. The man jerked his head round to stare at him for a second.

'He was in the dickens of a hurry for

some reason,' said Tanner after a second or so, 'He asked for his thirty shillings, and I gave them him. I wasn't exactly talkative myself. I hadn't much chance to inquire just where he was taking the trunk. Anyway, I was supposed to know, and I was banking on the chance that the driver had not met the man who ordered the van.'

'Mary and I were waiting for you at your flat,' replied Alan. 'The trunk duly arrived, and was duly lodged in the flat. But,' he paused, watching the effect of his words — 'there was blood seeping through the trunk. We got the police. Warren was not quite dead, and before he died, he managed to convey the news that you were on a houseboat somewhere in Hammersmith.'

'He wasn't dead!' Tanner echoed the words.

Alan continued grimly, savouring the irony of the moment:

'No! And his last words, spoken before two reliable witnesses, intimated that you killed him. That would be powerful testimony in court, Tanner. And I think that a jury would come to the conclusion you pulled that trigger.'

'I've told you I don't intend to go before any court,' muttered Tanner.

'I can't see anything else,' said Alan sombrely. 'A man has been killed — in self-defence admittedly — but the police will not rest until the case is settled legally.'

'They needn't find me!' snapped Tanner. 'We've eluded them. I can disappear. I may tell you I know a few dozen ways of taking on a new identity. Only fools are caught. The devil of it all is that I can't risk going into a court. No doubt I would be acquitted of murder and completely exonerated along with dear Pamela, but other things might come to light, which might earn me a goodish stretch. You will know that, Shaw! I'd sooner disappear than risk it.'

'Perhaps, but Pamela can't disappear,' retorted Alan. 'And then the police will question us and watch us like hawks. It is an impossible situation. Far better to have it completely cleared up.'

'That's what you think,' sneered Tanner.

'Do you think the police will be merely amused when they learn I was blackmailing Warren?'

'Hardly. It will not be your only crime. Mary and I met two police officers who were seeking to question you about your possession of forged money. They had called at your flat.'

Tanner started again.

'How the devil — ' He paused, breathing heavily. 'Odd notions occur to the police,' he said.

'I think it was more than a notion. They'd received anonymous information, I believe.'

'Oh. Anonymous, eh? A squeaker! Well, that is interesting — very interesting. And it strengthens my determination. The police are not going to see me again, if I can help it. You can trot along with your story of self-defence, and see if Pamela can be cleared, but I'm vanishing into thin air.'

'Oh, no,' said Alan grimly. 'We're going to Scotland Yard. If you see the inside of a prison for a few years, that will be a benefit to Pamela, and other girls like her.'

Tanner laughed coarsely.

'I wonder if Pam would prefer to jog along with me. Life would be very exciting, Pam.'

Mary felt the girl at her side stiffen.

'I'd hate *that* sort of excitement.' Pamela nearly choked on the words. 'What a fool I've been! Oh, Alan, take me home!'

'That is just like a woman,' sneered Tanner. 'Excitement has to be safe and pretty. My dear Pam, you disappoint me. I thought you could offer me a few thrills. You seemed daring enough in our many talks.'

Alan had to fight an inclination to smash his fist into the other's face. He maintained his vice-like grip on Tanner's arm, and pressed his fingers into the muscle until the fellow winced.

Alan half rose in the swaying taxi and managed to slide along the small glass panel so that he could speak to the driver.

'Take us to Scotland Yard, driver.'

The man nodded. As a London taxi man, life behind the wheel had long ceased to surprise him.

'You're a fool, Shaw.' gritted Tanner. 'You had better let me free.'

'Indeed. Don't you realise you're a menace to the community and to women in particular?'

'Put me in the dock and I'll smear Pamela's name over every sensational newspaper in the country. I'll swear she was my mistress, and that she enjoyed killing Warren. I'll say she helped me place Warren in the trunk. I'll swear she wanted to mutilate the body. I . . . '

'Shut up!' snapped Alan.

'I mean it!' panted Tanner. 'You'd better realise what it means. Pamela might not get out of the affair scot-free — as you seem to expect.'

'You swine!' said Alan softly. 'I'd like to kill you with my bare hands!'

'Stop the taxi and let me out,' said Tanner rapidly. 'You've been very helpful. Got me out of a tight corner. The police will wonder if I ever went down to the houseboat. And thanks for the information about the cops looking for dud money.'

'You are going straight into Scotland

Yard,' stated Alan.

'You'll risk Pamela's name and reputation?'

'I'll trust to the police to stop your game!'

Tanner went suddenly limp.

'You win, Shaw. Curse everything! It seems I'm booked for it now,' he whined.

Alan was grimly silent. The man's voice seemed suddenly tired, hopeless, but his plight aroused no sympathy in Alan's heart. Suddenly Tanner began pleading. The taxi was well into the City, now, speeding down the broad streets beneath the bright lamp standards.

'Pam, persuade your brother to let me get out of this taxi. Give me a sporting chance to dodge the police.'

But Pamela was silent. Mary's hatred of Fred Tanner had not diminished. She felt glad at last he was being brought to justice. She remembered Evelyn Torrance and had no pity for the creature beside her.

Alan looked out through the window at the passing shop fronts and porticos.

'Nearly there,' he muttered.

And then Tanner uncoiled from his limpness, like an animal suddenly aroused. He jerked his arm free from Alan's grasp, and acted furiously, like a madman struggling to escape. Thrusting his free hand into the breast of his coat for a tense second he fumbled, and then crushed down on Alan with all his force. As Alan threw him back into his seat, he snatched out a revolver and stabbed it before Alan's eyes.

'Thanks for the ride,' grated Tanner. 'We've gone far enough. This is Warren's gun. I don't suppose you realised my overcoat had a holster under the armpit. Trouble was you've been gripping the only hand which could get at this gun quickly, Mr. Wiseacre Shaw.'

Alan froze, staring at the gun-barrel less than six inches from his face. If Tanner pressed the trigger, the bullet would pulp his brain.

Tanner moved warily, like a cunning fighter in the ring. He managed to slide the glass panel back and speak to the driver.

'Stop at once.'

The gun moved in a slow, menacing

arc, covering Mary and Alan. The taxi braked steadily. Tanner rocked as the vehicle swayed to a standstill.

'Now I'm going.' Tanner was enjoying hugely the success of his trick. His conceit persuaded him there was nothing impossible to him. He waited until the taxi finally halted. He opened the door with one hand. 'I'm going. Pay the driver for me, Shaw,' he taunted.

'Wait, Fred. I — I want to come with you!'

Pamela Shaw spoke impulsively. Mary, trembling with the tenseness of the situation, felt a wave of amazement sweep over her.

'I love — you — Fred — in spite of — everything!' Pamela uttered the words in a strained, earnest tone. 'I'm sorry, Fred, I didn't mean it when I said I was a fool. It is you with whom I want to be all the time. You are right. It is excitement I want with you.'

He paused with the taxi door open, and laughed bombastically.

'So you still want to be with me! I knew you couldn't feel any other way about me.

Why shouldn't you go with me? In which case I could do with this taxi . . . '

Alan said urgently: 'Pam, don't be a fool.'

Feeling bitterly futile before the threat of the gun, he watched and wondered at the crazy infatuation that was leading his sister to run off with a crook, a blackmailer, a murderer virtually.

Tanner was covering the taxi-driver, who turned and saw the evil glitter of the snub-nosed barrel. ''Ere,' he began, but broke off as Tanner swung the gun meaningfully towards him. A bead of sweat showed on the taxi-man's forehead. He wiped his mouth with the back of a hand that trembled.

For a second Alan nearly risked a leap at Tanner. He calmly considered whether the man would dare to shoot and attract attention. But the taxi had drawn up in a quiet back street, and Tanner sensed his intention.

'Don't try a trick. I would shoot to get away. But that isn't necessary. Get out of this cab, Shaw — and my dear Mary. I need it to continue my journey with

Pamela. Get out!'

There was nothing else for it under the threat of the gun. Alan delayed as long as he dared until Tanner hissed: 'Hurry up, confound you! Do you want me to crack the butt on Miss Calvin's head?'

Reluctantly Alan descended from the cab, helping Mary. They stood in the roadway. Tanner quickly climbed into the cab with Pam. He leaned forward and placed the gun-muzzle beneath the driver's ear. The man flinched at the cold touch of the steel.

'Never mind Scotland Yard, my friend! Drive on! I'll give you orders later — and you needn't worry about your money — or your life, if you're a good boy!'

As the cab started off, Alan shouted desperately. He could see Pamela's white face staring straight ahead.

'Pam! Get out before it's too late! Pam!'

And then the taxi went down the road with a surge of power and disappeared round the corner.

6

Phone Call

'Pamela must be utterly mad to accompany a swine like that!'

Alan spoke bitterly, incensed by his failure, exasperated by his sister's folly.

'It doesn't make sense,' said Mary slowly. 'I'm sure she really hates him — now. I could have sworn she meant it when she asked you to take her home. And at the same time, I'm sure she didn't mean those words to Tanner about loving him.'

'I should have killed him and flung him in the river!' raged Alan.

They walked slowly down the road. He was sardonically aware of the futility of walking helplessly along a London street while his sister was speeding through the night with a man wanted for murder.

'We're still going to Scotland Yard,' he announced. 'I'll tell them everything.'

Cinemas were emptying as they walked rapidly through streets to reach the most famous police headquarters in the world. Alan asked to be shown to Detective-Inspector Lumley, and they waited for a few minutes in a glass-partitioned office. Lumley entered and sat down. He heard Alan out in silence, and then nodded his grey head.

'Just a few minutes ago I received a call from my sergeant who is searching for Tanner down at Hammersmith. He says he cannot find the man.' Detective-Inspector Lumley gave a curt nod. 'I'm not surprised after hearing your story.'

'You must understand, Inspector. I was anxious to help my sister. We were lucky enough to find them running away from the houseboat. When Tanner said my sister had shot Warren, I was astounded. I had only one thought, and that was to get her away and hear her story.'

Lumley smiled,

'Of course, a defending counsel would have little difficulty in proving that Merson Warren was shot in self-defence. But we must find Miss Shaw and Tanner.

I may say that we will do our best to get Mr. Tanner a prison sentence on other counts. He is a clever 'con' man, and worse, but not so clever to have avoided our suspicions altogether.'

'I'd give a lot to see that swine behind prison bars,' said Alan. 'What I can't understand is how Pamela can condescend to associate with him. Do you think you'll get Tanner soon?'

'He seems to be clever,' said Detective-Inspector Lumley carefully.

'Do you mean he stands a chance of staying clear — free to do what he likes?' exclaimed Alan in surprise.

'You have been an intelligence officer,' said the policeman. 'You know that many things happen which never reach newspaper headlines, and I can tell you that many thieves, rogues, and even murderers successfully elude the law for years. If Tanner vanishes, he will not be the first crook to disappear and take on a new identity. I tell you this so that you may know the plain truth; but it may happen that we'll get Tanner pretty soon.'

There was dismissal in the way Lumley

rose from his desk.

Alan escorted Mary home to her flat. She lived near Regents Park, a few minutes walk from her hat shop. Stars were studding the night-blue sky. A breeze, high in the heavens, had chased the gloomy clouds away.

'Where are you going now?' Mary whispered.

They stood on the doorstep, and he smiled down to her.

'I'd be after Pamela if I had the faintest idea where Tanner has taken her. As it is I'll go along to a small hotel where they know me pretty well. It is the Hampton Grill, near Holborn. I'd like to see you in the morning, Mary. You've been a great friend. You've really tried to help me with Pamela. I shall be forever grateful.'

Earlier, she had told him about her hat shop, and now it occurred to her as a useful rendezvous.

'You could see me tomorrow at my shop,' she said. 'I'd like to help you beat Tanner. If anything happens, please phone me.'

She left him, running to the lift with a

sudden beating of her heart.

She felt worn out as she entered her flat. The day's events had left her feeling utterly tired. She undressed, and then climbed into her bed and was almost instantly asleep.

The phone at her bedside seemed to jangle for a long time before she dragged herself out of the deep sleep that engulfed her. She glanced at the clock. Nearly three hours had passed since she got into her bed. It seemed less than three minutes. Who on earth was phoning in the middle of the night?

It might be Alan! She grabbed the instrument.

'Hello, Is that you, Alan?'

A girl's voice answered. It was a voice fraught with fear.

'Hello, Mary. This is Pamela Shaw speaking. Listen to me, Mary! I hate Fred Tanner.'

'Why did you go with him?'

Mary could detect a sudden fierceness in Pamela's voice.

'It was an impulse. I suddenly knew how much I detested him, and hated the

88

thought that he was going to escape. You know I told him I loved him. Well, I don't. I hate him! But I thought if I went along with him I could keep track of him until the right moment and then I'd phone Alan and he'd get the police.'

'But, Pamela, if he suspects you, you'll be in danger!' exclaimed Mary.

'Perhaps,' retorted Pamela over the wire. Her voice held something of her old spirit. 'Look here, Mary, if he catches me at this phone, he will suspect. I've only a minute or so. Get Alan, and bring him to this address — with the police, if he wants it that way. The address is 10, Elm Crescent, off the Wiltshire Road. Tanner is planning to lie low here, I think.'

'Alan is staying at a hotel,' exclaimed Mary. 'Don't worry, Pamela. We'll get the police and have Tanner rounded up.'

'For heaven's sake, hurry! Fred Tanner expects me to stay this night as his wife,' Pamela's voice trembled a little. 'I have made several excuses to get away from him — I can't hold out any longer! Two horrible old people keep this house. They are an old man and his wife. They seem ghastly, drunken people too! God knows how Fred Tanner persuades them to do his bidding, but they seem glad to have him. They — '

All at once Pamela's voice ceased. Mary heard a loud metallic click; the line went suddenly dead. She spoke urgently into the telephone several times, but received no reply.

Obviously, Pamela had been torn away from the telephone! Someone had discovered her — Tanner or one of his dreadful cronies.

Pamela had acted courageously in accompanying Fred Tanner. No doubt she had clutched at the wild idea of keeping track of the man who had deceived her. But it was a crazy, dangerous game.

And now what had happened to the girl?

As Mary rapidly flicked the pages of her telephone directory, she imagined the girl in some strange house combing the same pages to get her phone number. Pamela Shaw's infatuation must have given place to bitter hate, for only a strong emotion could be prompting her to carry out her plan.

In a sense it was one way of ensuring that Fred Tanner did not vanish, and in which Pamela could obtain some sort of revenge. For she must be feeling furious, thinking of the way in which she had been duped.

Mary wondered for a moment why Pamela had not phoned the police, but perhaps she had turned instinctively to the girl who would be able to contact the brother who now seemed a tower of strength in her adversity.

Mary got through to the night staff of the Hampton Grill, and said she wanted to speak urgently to Mr. Alan Shaw.

After a short time Alan's voice came through.

'Alan, I've just had a phone call from Pamela. She has been taken to an address off the Wiltshire Road. The place is 10, Elm Crescent. She doesn't care for Tanner — in fact she hates him, and she seized this chance of keeping on his track. But we must hurry. Someone took away the phone from Pamela as she was speaking to me.'

91

'The wild little idiot!' cried Alan Shaw,
'She did not phone the police. I think she felt keen to let you know the reason for her actions, and she knows you will do everything in the world to get Tanner caught.'

'You bet I will. And the police will have to be informed. Personally I'd like to smash Tanner with my own hands, but the law regards him as a human being. I'll ring Scotland Yard, and then set off for Elm Crescent.'

'I want to come with you, Alan,' cried Mary.

'No, Mary, you must not! It's dangerous.'

'But I hate Fred Tanner, You know that.'

'Mary, you're great, but stay where you are. Now I've got to ring the police.'

And Mary's telephone went dead.

She replaced the receiver and hurriedly dressed. She was determined to see the final roundup and the rescue of Pamela. To see Fred Tanner brought to justice would be a pleasure she did not intend to miss, and also, she might be able to help.

She flung off her tiredness in the excitement of the moment. She climbed into a serviceable tweed costume and brogues. She wound a gay turban round her black hair, and within a few minutes was ready to leave the flat.

Only then did she realise that Alan's last words on the phone had been very abrupt, and that he would not expect her at the Hampton Grill. More than that, Alan would leave the hotel as quickly as possible. Even now he would be on his way to Elm Crescent. He would have phoned the police, too. But Mary's chin was set determinedly. She felt she had put Alan on Fred Tanner's track, and she wanted to be in at the kill. Once she had even thought of killing Fred Tanner herself, and the tragedy of Evelyn Torrance's death still roused her to fury.

Mary made a snap decision. She would take a taxi to the street off the Wiltshire Road and join Alan there.

She left her flat and ran to the cab rank two blocks distant. Quickly she found a taxi driver and gave him the address. She climbed into the taxi and sat to regain her breath as it moved off.

The short journey through the quiet streets was quickly completed. The taxi slowed and stopped. The driver turned in his seat, and spoke through the small aperture behind him.

'Here, Miss. Do you want me to wait?'

Looking out, Mary saw two other cars. One was obviously a taxi. The other she guessed must be a police car. Alan and the police had arrived!

She paid off her driver. Alan, she felt sure, would see her home.

Mary ran along the pavement towards the stationary taxi. There was no other occupant except the driver. She looked up at the gaunt, three-storeyed houses. A burly, uniformed policeman standing on the stone steps leading to one house told her that this was number 10. She ran towards him.

'I should like to see Mr. Alan Shaw — is he here?'

The policeman eyed her shrewdly. He came closer to her.

'What is it you want, Miss?'

'I'd like to see Mr. Shaw. I want to

know if Tanner is caught, and if Pamela Shaw is safe.'

Even as the policeman stood in silence, the door of the house opened and a tall figure came down the steps. It was Alan. He came towards Mary with a haggard look in his eyes.

'Hello, Mary. So you didn't stay in bed!'

'How could I? Have the police got Tanner? Is Pamela safe?'

There was cold anger in his lean face.

'The house is empty. The birds have flown. Tanner and his friends evidently took Pamela away the moment they caught her at the telephone.'

'Oh, Alan! How terrible for her!'

'Detective-Inspector Lumley is inside the house now. They are looking for a clue, but I don't think they'll find much.' Alan turned to the constable. 'This lady is my friend, and the friend of my sister. I've told Inspector Lumley I'm going.'

The constable watched them cross to Alan's waiting taxi.

Inside the cab, Alan brought out a scrap of paper.

'Pamela left this note. I kept it from Lumley's view. The note was hidden under the telephone stand. Evidently Pam managed to hide it in the confusion.'

Mary read the note. It was a scribble in pencil and was addressed to no one.

★   ★   ★

'They are taking me to Pearly's house. I've heard them speaking before about someone called Pearly. I have no idea where the place is. Tanner threatens to kill me the next time I squeal to the police, but I'm not afraid. If the police find this note please, please try to discover Pearly's.'

★   ★   ★

The note was unsigned, except for a scrawled letter 'P'.

'You see, Mary, I cannot show Lumley this note,' said Alan harshly. 'We are hounding Tanner. He might carry out his threat. He might kill Pamela if he suspects she left this note, and he will suspect if the police know about Pearly and come tearing along to his house, I'll have to contact Tanner and pay him to set Pamela free.'

7

Ted Leesing's Double-Cross

The taxi was speeding down the road, making towards the Marylebone district: Alan was seeing Mary home for the second time that night. But he was in a grim mood. She longed to comfort this tall lean man. In some inexplicable way she felt he needed 'mothering', although he was so self-reliant.

'I'll contact Tanner somehow,' Alan stated. 'Pamela has got to be rescued from him. Money is the one thing Tanner understands.'

Yet he knew it would not be easy if Fred Tanner was determined to go underground.

'I'll get in touch with a private investigator who will work with less noise than the police.'

'Won't it be difficult for Pamela when the police question her about Merson

Warren's death?' asked Mary.

He nodded grimly.

'It will be rotten. Even without Tanner, the police will have to make a charge, though there can be no doubt she will be acquitted. Even Tanner would be exonerated on that score because there is no doubt Merson Warren intended murder. But Tanner would be in a sticky position on other counts, if the police can find enough evidence to show he was practising blackmail. Then the police will not have forgotten that Tanner may be making or distributing forged money. They'll do their best to make a case against him, and Tanner knows it. He's very much afraid, or he'd risk an appearance in court which would clear him so far as Merson Warren's death is concerned.'

★   ★   ★

When Mary finally went to rest that night, she found sleep harder to obtain than she thought possible. Mad thoughts of a captive Pamela Shaw haunted her mind. At last sleep came and Mary's troubled thoughts vanished.

The next morning she went to her shop for she was too astute a woman to neglect her business for long. A few minutes after she had opened with the help of her assistants, Alan walked in.

'Hello, Mary.' His dark eyes held an observant glint. He walked along to her small office. 'You're looking extraordinarily alert this morning. Personally, I feel as though I've lost some sleep.' He was noting with admiration the chic lines of her new morning frock. Her dark hair gleamed, falling silkily along her neck.

'I always dress the part for business,' retorted Mary. She sat down. 'What are you doing about Pamela? If there's anything I can do — '

He hitched his trousers and sat on the arm of her easy chair. The hotel staff must have pressed his decently-cut suit. He was well-groomed, showing no sign of his tussle with Tanner and his taxi-travelling.

'Thanks, Mary. But there's little you can do. I simply popped in to let you know I'm on my way to see a private investigator. Afraid I can't stay long. I wish I could.'

Even so they talked slowly, intimately for a few minutes.

And then he left.

Hardly had Alan left the street when Mary was visited by another man, who had certainly not arrived to buy a lady's hat.

He entered, a cigarette drooping from his slack mouth. He glanced round warily, as if suspecting trickery from even a hat-stand. Mary's assistant decided that here was a nervous gentleman desirous of buying a hat for his wife — a bullying wife, most probably.

The assistant could not have been further from the truth. Ted Leesing had never possessed a legal wife.

'I want to see Miss Calvin,' he told the girl, and he was shown to Mary's office, where she was busy at the accounts. She was surprised, and inquired his business.

'You're Miss Calvin?' said the man. He essayed a smile, but no smile could chase the chronic disgruntled expression from his face. 'I got your name from the night porter at Tanner's flat.'

Mary jerked upright in the swivel seat.

'What do you know about Tanner? Why do you want to see me?'

Ted Leesing made a pacifying motion with his hands.

'Let me have my say, Miss Calvin. Now — I don't like Tanner. He did me wrong once over a deal. I had to be pally with him afterwards, and he's got such a fine opinion of himself that he's forgotten the dirt he handed me.'

'Do you know where Fred Tanner has gone?'

'I don't, but I got the whole yarn from the night porter about the murder, I told the night porter I was a newspaper reporter. Swallowed it, too, he did. That was after the police had left. I got your name and address as well. That blinking porter hadn't missed a word.'

'He was questioned with us by the police.'

'You see, Miss,' continued Ted Leesing, 'I was waiting for the cops turning up at Tanner's flat. I saw you and the gent speak to the sergeant and the constable. That was before the van brought that old trunk.'

'Why should you be waiting?' Mary asked curiously.

Ted Leesing scowled.

'I knew they'd come, that's all. Now let me say what I want to say. I saw you and the gent speak to the first cops. I was inside a phone booth across the way — better than walking up and down. Well, I wondered what Tanner wanted with the old trunk. Then when Lumley from the Yard arrived, I knew there was something queer. As I say, I finally got the whole thing pitched to me later by the night porter, though I can tell you it was a good bit later. I didn't want to meet Lumley.'

'I suppose the night porter knew my address as well as my name?' remarked Mary.

'Yes, he's a born nosey-parker — or the job's made him that way. Now I've read this morning's papers — only one has the news and that's just a few lines in the stop-press. Nothing much there. Just about a body being found in a trunk.'

103

Mary nodded.

'They haven't got Tanner,' declared Ted Leesing. 'He committed the murder, didn't he? Why did he send that trunk to his flat? Did he intend to dispose of it later?'

'I still don't see much reason for your visit,' said Mary coldly. 'I can tell you that the dead man was shot in self-defence, and that the trunk was sent to Tanner's flat by mistake. Now have you anything else to say?'

The other twisted his mournful lips.

'Yes. I know that Mr. Shaw is worried about his sister. The night porter had all that part of the business pat, too. He told me that young feller has a sister who went off with Tanner. Let me tell you, Miss, that if she's gone with Tanner, she's gone with a slimy snake.'

'And what else?' asked Mary impatiently.

'Just this. I want to see Tanner doing a stretch, and I don't intend to be with him. I've got my plans. I'm saying nothing about them. But I'm scramming to the north today, where I've got a hideout that'll last me a year, if I want it. Now I can't go to the cops. I've got one reason for coming to see you, and it's simple: I want to tell you a lot of things about Tanner so when you next see the cops you'll have some hot information. Want to hear about his roulette tables at Peolozzi's? Want to hear about his splosh? That dud money?'

Mary could hardly understand the man's jargon, but she suddenly tensed as a thought struck her.

'I'd like to hear about Pearly's house,' she said quickly.

Ted Leesing sat with a blank expression.

'Pearly?' he said.

Mary thought quickly, her mind racing over the facts. She decided there was no reason why she should not speak more freely to this man.

'Fred Tanner has taken Alan Shaw's sister to a house owned by someone called Pearly. Now Alan is very anxious to find Pamela, and I think he would pay a good sum for information which would lead him to Pearly's house.'

Ted Leesing smiled furtively.

'So Tanner is staying at Pearly's house! You ask me if I know the place? I say I do. You've hit on the right guy, Miss, when you ask that question.'

'Show Alan to the place and he'll pay you.'

Ted Leesing shook his head firmly.

'No, Miss. That young feller might think I'd be better off talking to the cops. He's that sort. He'd bring the cops into it at the first few words. I got enough worries coming here.'

'I can promise you that Alan Shaw will not approach the police.'

'Nothing doing, Miss.'

'Do you know the whereabouts of this house — Pearly's house?' asked Mary impatiently.

'I sure do. Pearly — well, she's known to a few blokes like me.'

'So *he's* a *woman*! Please give me the address.'

Ted Leesing considered for an appreciable moment, a cunning look in his watery eyes.

'Tell you what, I'll show you the house

for a few quid. You're a girl, and I know how to handle skirts. But that young feller, Mr. Shaw, I'm not dealing with him. Oh, no!'

Mary hesitated, only another few seconds. Then she rose from her seat. She reached for her camel-haired coat, slipped it on and tied the belt.

'Take me to this house,' she said determinedly. 'I'll give you your few pounds.'

Ted Leesing gave his travesty of a smile once more.

★ ★ ★

He accompanied Mary to a dingy street in Limehouse. Mary had hired the taxi and now she paid the driver while Ted Leesing stared blankly down the mean street. There was a peculiar, dilapidated air about the buildings lining the street. Mary received the impression that the medley of houses was long accustomed to dirt, misuse and odd inhabitants.

Ted Leesing stood still, as if reluctant to proceed another yard. He watched the taxi drive off before he spoke, and even then his voice was a hoarse whisper.

'You'll find Pearly's house through the second alley on the left. You'll find a door. Big, wide — looks like a church door, but it ain't. That's Pearly's.'

'Who is Pearly?' asked Mary.

'She's a dame you'd hate to meet. She's been 'inside' a few times. She's fat — but she's as strong as a man. She's usually half tight — or more than half! She can swill whisky like she had a hundred year thirst. Pearly gets a cut off nearly every racket you can imagine. I wouldn't tell a nice girl like you half the things Pearly has her fingers in. If your friend is in there, God help her! Pearly is an old swine! That house's cellars could tell a strange story or two, I'll guarantee!'

'But why don't the police do something about people like that?' asked Mary, astonished.

He chuckled.

'If the cops lifted everybody who looked shady, the prisons would be filled a hundred times over and then some. Now I'm going.' He gnawed his lips uncertainly.

'Coming? This place isn't healthy for a girl like you.'

Mary looked round the sordid street. Ted Leesing shuffled impatiently. He was turning, his hands stuck in the pockets of his creased overcoat, when two big men came round a corner. Both wore florid checked suits and bowler hats. There was an unpleasant glint in their eyes. Ted started instinctively, knowing well what their purposeful strides towards him foretold.

Mary did not scent danger as quickly as Ted Leesing. She had seen some odd-looking individuals in these grimy streets and she realised this was a part of London with which she was totally unfamiliar.

But when Ted Leesing tried suddenly to evade the grasp of one of the newcomers, Mary's heart jumped in sudden terror. He was too late in his reaction. His arms were gripped. A thick voice rasped a threat, and sheer fright brought paralysis to Leesing's limbs.

Mary found her arms suddenly pinioned, her attacker having fingers like

109

steel. She screamed in terror, but a dirty hand was immediately clamped over her mouth.

She was forced down the road, swiftly, in spite of her furious struggles. Unknown to her, Leesing was suffering a similar fate, but without her spirited resistance.

The Limehouse street lay quiet and depressing, indifferent to the scuffle. If any of its inhabitants observed the brief affair, they declined to take even the slightest interest.

And then the two men took their captives through the second alley on the left, and the street was quiet and deserted once more.

8

Trapped!

To Mary Calvin the struggle with her captor was a grim period of futile effort and confused impressions. She hardly realised why she had been attacked, but somehow her intuition told her that Fred Tanner was the instigator.

She was carried through an archway and then through a wide doorway, and after that her captor hauled her down a long, dank flight of spiral stone stairs. Behind her, Ted Leesing was manhandled along, paralysed with fear. Occasionally a terrified whimper escaped him, and once Mary heard the thud of a blow, followed by a quick sobbing intake of breath.

Eventually they were bundled into a large cellar with a vaulted roof where a foul, musty odour permeated the air.

The two men stared sourly at their captives. One slowly brought out a large clasp knife, which had a blade whetted to razor sharpness. They seemed to be waiting. Mary sat up defiantly and arranged her skirt. Her dusky captor grinned unpleasantly, blinking his amber eyes.

And then the man for whom they were evidently waiting came into the cellar, switching on the electric light.

Fred Tanner was as immaculate as ever. His suit fitted him perfectly. One might have thought he had just taken it from a wardrobe, and the elegant turnout was adequate testimony to a product that had once cost Tanner plenty. A white handkerchief showed silkily at his breast pocket and Mary glimpsed the gold wristwatch beneath his cuff.

He closed the cellar door behind him, and then, thrusting his hands into his pockets, advanced towards Mary and Ted Leesing. But the nonchalance had vanished from Fred Tanner's face — the mouth was set and cruel, the eyes narrowed

'I don't understand this,' he said slowly. 'How did you know where to find me?'

He seemed to be immersed in thoughts of his own and spoke in little more than a whisper

'The police will soon be here,' Mary flung at him.

'Let me out of here, Tanner!' choked Ted Leesing. 'Don't you believe this dame! I brought her down here. She wanted to find Pearly's house. The cops don't come into this! You know I wouldn't have anything to do with the cops!'

'How did you know I'd be here?' Tanner suddenly shouted at Mary.

She remained silent, thinking desperately. If she mentioned Pamela leaving a note in the empty house at Elm Crescent, Tanner might carry out his threat to kill her. Perhaps it would be wiser not to inform him that Alan Shaw knew of Pamela's detention at Pearly's house, and was now trying to find a private investigator who might help.

'What made you come here?' Tanner ground out.

Mary said nothing and Tanner's eyes blazed with fury. He took a quick step forward and raised his hand.

'This skirt knew you had the girl at Pearly's, Tanner!' shrieked Ted Leesing. 'Don't, Fred, don't . . . '

Tanner relaxed and made an effort to regain his old mocking attitude.

'I'll get to know everything soon enough,' he said. 'And I know one thing, Ted. You tried to give me away to the cops over the dud notes. That wasn't nice, Ted.'

'What do you mean, Fred?' Ted Leesing faltered. Great beads of sweat started upon his forehead. 'You know I wouldn't do that! I swear it!'

And Ted Leesing was dragged out, shouting incoherent terror-stricken sentences.

Several hours later a patrolling policeman discovered the body of a man in Hyde Park. He was extended upon the grass, his hat tilted forward over his eyes. Only the great red stain seeping through the newspaper on his chest told that here was more than a mere sleeper.

Even in death, Ted Leesing's mouth seemed twisted in a cold bitter smile.

★ ★ ★

Tanner came over to Mary, and pulled her roughly to her feet.

'I'm going to have the truth from you,' he sneered. 'It was lucky for me that I happened to be up in the tower when you came down the road.'

Mary tried to steady herself. She did not speak.

'A quaint feature of Pearly's house is that tower,' went on Tanner as if taunting the girl gave him back his old feeling of superiority. 'One has a commanding view of both ends of the street. Pearly finds it convenient when the police make an appearance — which isn't frequent.'

He gripped her arms, and she struggled.

'I'm taking you to see dear Pamela. That is what you want, isn't it? Now don't struggle, my dear.'

Mary retaliated by kicking his shins. Tanner's eyes glinted with anger and pain, and he shook the girl until her head swam and her struggles subsided.

'I am still very fond of the ladies,' he sneered. 'Though recent events are tending to cramp my activities. If you try to struggle again I shall extract the penalty like this!'

Exerting his strength he brought Mary close to him and kissed her passionately.

She struggled in fury, incensed at his touch.

'Leave me alone, you brute!' she cried.

Tanner raised his hand to strike but changed his mind. With a little difficulty he once more embraced the girl. Then he slackened his grasp.

'There, my pretty one. Now be quiet or I shall kiss you again.'

Mary trembled, breathing quickly. Tanner took her arm, watching her narrowly, and led her to the cellar door. Mary went without protest. She knew that she must now keep cool and use her wits.

Outside the cellar ran a passage. Mary stared along the dim corridor, wondering where Pamela was in this terrible house. Tanner retained a strong grip upon her arm, and propelled her along. Walls of crumbling brick and stone, encompassed the pair as they moved away from the solitary light and approached another door at the end of the passage.

Evidently the door was locked on the other side, for Tanner stopped and gave a peculiar double-knock. In the short pause that followed, he said, 'You will find Pamela behind this door enjoying the adventurous life she professes to like. She is not alone. I shall soon learn how you came to know of Pearly's house, and just how dangerous you are.'

The cellar door was opened by an aged man of hideous visage. The pouched, wrinkled face framed a pair of dull, sombre eyes, which showed not a spark of life. Mary screamed at his very appearance, but Tanner pushed her forward. The old man shuffled to one side.

'You got another beauty, Tanner!' slobbered the old man.

'Another, Slowther,' agreed Tanner, and he moved into the cellar.

The man called Slowther locked the door behind them and then turned to leer at Mary. He fastened his evil eyes on the girl as if she were an exhibit,

Mary, horrified by the grotesque old man, was equally repulsed when she found herself staring at an old hag of a woman who was apparently the man's wife. She remembered Pamela's mention on the phone of the old drunken degenerates who had kept the house in Elm Crescent. Evidently this was the same horrible pair.

And then she saw Pamela.

The girl was but a shadow of her former spirited self. She started to her feet as Mary entered and there was fear in her eyes. Pamela was pale and her hair disarranged. Her costume had been torn and there was a bruise on her cheek.

Mary knew Tanner had been ill-treating her and in her anger tugged at Tanner's grasp on her arm. He laughed and allowed her to go free and she ran at once to Pamela and hugged her.

'Oh, Pamela! What has he done to you?' she cried.

The other girl stared, pale and dry-eyed. She whispered:

'He has whipped me, Mary.'

'She has been enjoying an adventure with me,' retorted Tanner. 'I cannot be gentle with those who try to double-cross me. Please remember that, Mary, for I want you to speak the truth.'

And when Mary looked up she saw Tanner fondling a black leather whip. The whip was many thonged, with a short handle.

'Belonged to Pearly and heaven knows where she found it,' commented Tanner. 'How do you like it, Mary?'

'I think you are an unspeakable beast!'

'How original! Well, I intend to make you tell me how it happens you knew Pamela and I would be staying at Pearly's house.'

'You wouldn't dare use that!' choked Mary.

'I have used it. Pamela refused to stay with me during the night. I can't imagine why. Didn't she say she wanted adventure and that she loved me?' He was enjoying his mockery. 'So I tried the effect of a whip in quite the medieval manner. I rather think I should have lived in those days.'

'You should never have been born!' cried Mary.

'But I was, and I intend to live a great

deal longer too.' Suddenly his tone changed and he snapped: 'Now, where is Alan Shaw?' Does he know I'm hiding here? What about the police — did you tell them you were coming? And how did you know where to find me? I'm sure Leesing didn't know.'

'The police will be here soon!' said Mary.

She tried to make the brave words sound convincing, but Tanner only smiled and drew the thongs of the whip through his fingers.

'Lies! Why aren't they here now? How did you learn about Pearly's house? Where is Alan Shaw?'

'You're afraid of him!' retorted Mary.

In sudden fury Tanner swung the whip. The leather thongs sung through the air and wound round Mary's body like a living thing. She tried to force back her sudden scream of pain. Tanner recovered the whip with a jerk, which nearly overbalanced her, the lash plucking viciously at her clothing.

'I want the truth!' shouted Tanner. His face was livid, and Mary tensed herself for another blow.

'Why did you not arrive with Alan Shaw?' he snarled.

The long whip curled out and the torturing leather bit at Mary's legs. An involuntary scream rose to her lips and when the lashes fell away, blood appeared through the torn silk of her stockings. 'Don't, Fred, don't! I'll tell you!' screamed Pamela. 'I left a note under the phone at Elm Crescent. I put Pearly's name in it!'

'In spite of the thrashing I gave you after discovering you at the phone, you thought you could double-cross me again. I'll make you regret it, my girl!' He paused. 'How is it the police didn't see the note, Mary?' he asked.

Sick with pain and shock, Mary said faintly: 'The police did see the note. They'll soon be here. Why don't you let us go? Why don't you escape?'

'Take her coat off, Slowther,' ordered Tanner.

The old man moved with alacrity. Mary saw nothing but expectancy of enjoyment in a face that had seen all manner of evil.

The hag, though motionless, was enjoying the scene as much as the man. Her lined face was indescribably vicious. The sight of the ghastly pair sickened Mary.

'Mr. Tanner is no fool,' chuckled Slowther in admiration, and Fred Tanner snatched at a bottle of whisky from a table. His West-end manners had disappeared, and he drank from the bottle with a beast-like greed.

Pamela's cry momentarily deterred Tanner.

'Stop! Fred ... please ... I'll do anything ... please!' A sudden thought had struck her and breathlessly she cried, 'I wrote that I was afraid you'd kill me if you thought I'd squealed to the police. Perhaps Alan thought it was better not to show the police the note.'

Pamela then rushed towards Mary.

'Tell him the truth, Mary. He'll kill you!'

'Is that right?' demanded Tanner. 'Is that right, I say?'

But Mary remained obstinately silent, and the lash cut the air again. Tanner went berserk for a time. At length he desisted, panting with his exertions. Mary moaned mutely; he threatened her again. Words she could not control issued from her lips. She was beaten. She told Tanner what he wanted to know.

Tanner coiled the leather thongs round the stubby handle. He snatched again at the whisky bottle.

'So neither the police nor Alan Shaw know you are here,' he said harshly. 'But Shaw has the note which says we are hiding at Pearly's house.'

He paused to take a deep drink from the bottle. When he replaced it on the table, there was an unpleasant glint in his eyes. 'We shall have to make another blasted move,' he said. 'Shaw might easily find this house. Pearly has, I'll admit, something of a reputation in the criminal world.'

Adam Slowther and his hag exchanged glances, and Mary found their hostile gaze directed towards her. From vicious amusement their feelings had changed to the disturbing knowledge that their hideout was known.

'You should wring the necks of these

two beauties, Mr. Tanner,' growled Slowther. 'That's what I would do when I was your age. Make an end o' them, I say.'

Tanner brought out a heavy automatic, and handed it to Slowther.

'Keep guard on them while I have a pow-wow with Pearly about a new hideout, and be careful, you old fool. It's loaded. I intend to hand over two live girls to Pearly before we leave, but don't let that stop you shooting if they try anything dangerous.'

'Pearly will know what to do with two pretty girls!' cackled Mrs. Slowther, and suddenly the old woman laughed harshly and piercingly, with the hoarse note of some bird-of-prey exulting over its quarry.

Slowther found his task enjoyable. He was an old reprobate who had spent half his life in prison and did not realise there was any sort of life possible other than that of the habitual criminal. He held the automatic as if the task was a precious one.

But the two girls were cowed, and

made no attempt at resistance, and before many minutes had elapsed Tanner hurried back into the cellar.

He took the gun from Slowther.

'I have a treat in store for you, my dear young ladies,' he said, with a wolfish grin. 'You are going up to the tower to witness a little comedy — or shall we say, perhaps, tragedy? Who knows? At least you will have a balcony seat for the performance! Get up! Get up!'

The girls rose to their feet. Tanner gestured towards the door with his gun. 'Walk!' he commanded 'And be very, very careful, my dears. I have yet to experience the pleasure of shooting a lady in the back.'

As they reached the door, Tanner paused, a sardonic smile curving his lips.

'As a prologue, you will see Alan Shaw and a man who is presumably a private detective. They are standing with commendable caution, at the end of our elegant street.'

9

Alan Sees Red

Mary's heart leaped.

'Alan is here!' She turned to Pamela, and squeezed her arm reassuringly. Both girls felt a new hope surge through them. 'Alan is here!' repeated Mary, wildly almost unbelievingly.

Tanner motioned impatiently with his gun.

'Hurry! Hurry! Or I'll make an end of you now.'

How much of his threat was real, the girls did not know but they moved quickly out into the passage. It seemed wiser, at least, to obey. Somehow Alan would — must — turn the tables!

'I'm coming, Mr. Tanner!' grunted Slowther.

'Stay where you are, you old fool!' snapped Tanner. 'I'm taking Jesse with me.'

Jesse proved to be one of the two men

who had captured Mary and Leesing earlier. He was standing silently in the passage as Pamela and Mary came out. He moved up to Mary and clutched her arm. His eyes stared unseeingly ahead, inhuman and uncaring, he might have been a man of steel. Not one fleeting expression distorted his set and ruthless countenance.

Tanner hustled them along, thrust his automatic into his jacket pocket and gripped the black leather whip in his hand.

At the end of the cellar passage a spiral staircase with worn stone steps led upwards. Here, Jesse went on ahead and Tanner brought up the rear. After innumerable treacherous steps and several turns, they finally entered a narrow gallery leading to a shorter flight of stairs, which gave access to a round stone compartment resembling the top of a miniature lighthouse. In spite of the grime that coated the walls, the windows that ringed the tower were perfectly clean and two were actually open.

'There you are, my dear Pamela! See

for yourself how your gallant brother rushes to rescue his foolish sister, and her equally foolish friend.'

They did not heed Tanner's taunts. They ran to the windows, and stared down into the street.

Alan and his companion were now walking slowly towards the alley that gave entrance to Pearly's mysterious house.

Alan walked side by side with a lean, hard-faced man in a raincoat and slouch hat. The man's hat was pushed back from his brow. His hands were in his pockets.

There was something curiously deliberate about the men's tread. They approached very slowly, not with reluctance but with the deliberation of men who knew they were courting trouble. Alan's hands were rammed into his jacket pockets

Unlike the other man, he was hatless and coatless. His dark hair was ruffled and a single lock had fallen across his forehead.

'So the private cop has found Pearly's house for little Alan!' sneered Tanner.

His taunt broke the tense, tomb-like silence of the stone chamber.

Pamela wheeled, sudden fear in her grey eyes

'Why have you brought us up here?'

'Why not?' retorted Tanner calmly. 'Everything is under control. I thought you would like a bird's-eye view of the proceedings.'

He brought out the automatic, came closer to the window and levelled his arm. He took careful aim at the two advancing men now clearly visible in the street some sixty feet below.

'You can't! You can't!'

Mary's reaction was swift. As she cried, she sprang at Tanner's arm. She brought it down with ease.

Tanner smiled sardonically. Tensing his muscles, he flung the girl from him. Mary collapsed by the low wall, sick and breathless. The boy Jesse slipped suddenly forward and pinioned Pamela's arms in an iron grip.

Tanner said mockingly: 'I did not intend to shoot. As I said, everything is under control. I admit the opportunity was splendid, but a dead man lying on the pavement would attract the police even in this — er — untidy neighbourhood. Oh, no, my dears, all is well. Your brother has not brought the police, and tonight I shall really vanish — as a lone wolf this time. Now look — look my dears!' Tanner pointed down at the street. There was a sudden expectant note in his voice, and in spite of themselves, Mary and Pamela stared fixedly through the wide windows at the scene below.

Alan and his companion were now directly below the roof from which the tower projected. They continued their measured paces. Another few yards and they would be abreast the alley, which gave access to the house.

'Can you see Pearly's men hiding in the passageway on the other side of the street?' Tanner questioned triumphantly. 'They will close upon Alan and his friend as soon as they enter the alley. And, in addition, Shaw will find a hot reception waiting him behind the main door of the house. Much better than an obtrusive body in the street, is it not?' He chuckled. 'Murder is hardly my line, either. All I wish is to tie up the loose ends and start afresh, and that I'll be doing tomorrow.'

But Mary Calvin barely heard his boastful words. Slowly she had turned her head from the window to gaze in sudden fascination at the gun dangling in Tanner's right hand. The man himself was momentarily absorbed in the scene below. Behind her, a yard or two distant, stood Jesse. His ugly face was inscrutable.

A daring idea had seized her mind. She knew she must get rid of Tanner's gun. If, by sheer courage, Alan and his companion fought through the house to the tower, they would be faced by a gun firing through the only entrance and be shot dead in the gallery outside.

Mary acted upon the instant. She threw herself at the carelessly-held gun. It was so near, so temptingly easy to secure, she was certain she could not fail! Her fingers touched the automatic, clutched, and her hand closed determinedly round the barrel. A sudden twist before Tanner's grip could tighten, and she felt the gun leave the man's hand. The next moment it belonged to her and she backed wildly away from him.

Tanner came after her at once, his eyes furious.

Mary's heart was thumping madly. She had never held a gun in her life. She knew nothing of its mechanism. She was suddenly afraid Tanner would dispossess her of it. At all costs, he must not get the gun back again, and Alan must be warned. With a sudden flash of inspiration, Mary swung her arm sideways and flung the weapon through the open window.

The gun fell to the pavement with a crash and exploded. Alan and his companion spun round as if on pivots and with one accord their eyes jerked up to the tower. For a moment, clear behind the windows, they saw a girl struggling with a man.

'Let's make it a party, Defoe!' rapped Alan.

Mark Defoe was the survivor of a hundred violent brushes with the brethren of the underworld, not only in London, but in the States. A former rugger 'tackle' and one-time amateur boxing champion of his class, he thrived on what he called 'a bit of trouble'. And trouble was not long in arriving. Even as they approached Pearly's house, the door was flung open and four men tumbled out.

They had been posted by Tanner: ruffians of various sizes and indeterminable colour, ugly brutes whose many scars testified to their manner of living. They came with a purposeful rush, fists raised.

But Alan Shaw and Mark Defoe met them with scientific precision. Before setting out, Defoe had armed Alan and himself each with a short rubber truncheon, a useful weapon with a flexible handle and lead-weighted head. And this each now literally swung into action!

Alan and Defoe downed two men in a matter of seconds, the animal rush of the attackers contributing to their downfall. They ran straight into the accurate and unexpected resistance of their quarry. The two remaining thugs leaped away, pulling from their jacket pockets heavy clasp-knives which flicked open to show razor-keen blades. The man nearest to Alan poised his arm ready to throw the knife, his face convulsed with rage and fear. Alan fell to one knee and the weapon sliced over his head. The next moment Alan launched himself forward and butted his assailant squarely in the stomach. The man groaned and crumpled. Alan jerked his head smartly back and had the satisfaction of feeling it collide with his opponent's jaw. The man reeled and as he did so, Alan struck him once, scientifically, with his cosh.

Defoe's opponent had fared no better than had Alan's. Indeed, his passage from consciousness had been quicker and more expertly accomplished.

'Come on,' said Alan, and leaving their prostrate assailants, they ran for Pearly's house. As they ran, Alan felt cold fear clutch at his heart.

Mary in Tanner's power! Undoubtedly, the girl struggling in the tower had been Mary! Such agonising knowledge was like a blow to Alan and suddenly he knew how much the girl meant to him. It was a strange revelation. He wondered how he had been so blind to his own feelings. The sight of Mary struggling with Tanner aroused sudden killing fury. Even if Mary did not care for him with this same new intensity that he cared for her, he would protect her, come what may.

The two men stumbled on to a passage, which ran straight to the door leading to the spiral-stairs, and Alan, panting, led the journey aloft. He could hear Defoe scrambling after him in the gloom, and once Defoe shouted to him to beware an ambush. They went up and up the twisting stairs.

* * *

As the gun fell, Tanner literally shrieked with rage. He leapt forward and caught Mary by the throat. As if in a dream he heard the crack of the shot, the sound of running feet below . . . The girl struggled gamely, and, then suddenly, Tanner flung her aside. He rushed to the window and peered out — but what he hoped had not come to pass! The thugs concealed across the street had vanished at the sound of the shot! Silent professional knife-fighters and 'razor-boys' they preferred less exciting tasks than those of tackling opponents who might be noisily and effectively armed.

Gibbering in fury, Tanner saw his second line of defence overwhelmed, saw Alan and Defoe enter the house . . . He turned, his eyes ablaze with rage, whip in hand he advanced on the two girls. Pamela screamed, piercingly, terrifyingly. And then Tanner struck one, two, three times . . . He seemed on the point of madness. Mary flung herself upon his whip arm, but was hurled aside.

'Alan! Alan!' shrieked Pamela, suddenly. And as if in answer to a prayer, Alan Shaw burst into the room . . .

His dash carried him through the flailing whip. He closed with Tanner and wrenching the stocky handle from the man's hand, rocked Tanner on his heels with a right hook, which released every atom of fury he felt for the man. He flung the whip aside, and slammed another punishing blow to the man's mouth . . .

Mark Defoe who had been outdistanced by the younger man in climbing the stairs, entered the tower a few seconds after Alan, and shouted a sudden warning.

'Duck, Alan, *duck*!'

And then he hurled himself at Jesse.

But the broad-bladed knife had left the mulatto's hand hurled with speed and accuracy.

Alan dropped as the first syllable left Defoe's lips. It was a perfect example of lightning reaction based on years of calculated training.

The blade whipped over Alan's shoulder and there was a sudden dreadful thud . . .

Alan rose slowly to his feet with an ashen face. Fred Tanner looked stupidly down at the knife-haft protruding from his side. He seemed about to speak. A few heavy drops of blood ran down his jacket, spreading on the fabric in a quickly broadening stain.

Suddenly, Tanner fell back like a marionette whose guide-strings had snapped. There was a crash, a patter of broken glass — and Alan Shaw found himself gazing at a broken window through which rushed the cool evening air.

Mary ran to Alan with a cry and he caught and held her.

Mark Defoe took charge of Jesse who thrust up his hands and rolled his eyes. Defoe glanced at the shattered window, then looked at Alan.

'We'd better contact the police before someone finds his body,' he advised.

Alan nodded. 'I'll 'phone the police right away. We've a heck of a lot explaining to do. We need to tell them the full story right away, to protect ourselves from any repercussions of this mayhem.'

'And Pamela, too,' Mary said softly.

★   ★   ★

A few days later, Alan sat with Pamela and Mary in a secluded summerhouse in the garden at The Laurels.

Nothing but the drowsy murmur of insects disturbed the lazy afternoon. The trio did not speak. Alan was holding Mary's hand. In the distance a clock struck four.

Breaking the silence, Pamela said, 'I

think I'll see if tea is ready.' She rose and walked away.

'Do you think she will get over it quickly, Alan?' asked Mary anxiously. 'She has been so quiet all day.'

He smiled slowly. 'Pam will soon be her old self, I've no doubt. There are a number of ardent young men eager to call . . . '

'Merson Warren's death is still worrying me,' confessed Mary.

Alan frowned, and then smiled at her as he took her hand again.

'I've reason to believe it won't be as bad for Pamela as we might think. She is completely innocent and the law isn't harsh with innocent people.'

'And,' continued Mary, 'Slowther and Pearly got away, vanished into thin air?'

Alan smiled and looked into her steady grey eyes. 'The police are looking for them. I don't doubt they'll be caught eventually. And you will never get away from me, either, my darling. You know I love you, Mary. Do you love me?'

'Oh, Alan, you know very well I do. I think I've loved you from the first moment I saw you. And now I feel so safe with you and so exquisitely happy.'

There was no need for further words.

Alan drew Mary to him and put his arms around her. She smiled radiantly, with the passionate ecstasy of awakened love.

Part 2

Wayward Women

1

Blackmail

Denise Hansen, the first wayward woman to visit Wilderhouse during that horrible week, had the wickedness of greed. She was driving through the night to extract from a wealthy man the price of her silence. Only when she was near the massive porticos of Wilderhouse did she hesitate. Blackmail was a fiendish business. She tried to justify herself: Floyd Paget was a swine. He had brought misery to a dozen or more beautiful young women.

Now he must pay for his callous follies in hard cash.

When she was shown into his study and he rose from his wing chair to greet her, she saw that he was as handsome as ever. Not long ago, she remembered, she'd had an adolescent infatuation for this middle-aged man . . . until she had learned how he treated women. Oh, he was courtly enough to begin with, and that grey-touched hair of his was disarming. It was only when one noticed those full, sensuous lips and the quartz-cold eyes that one sensed his cruel and weirdly passionate nature.

An inscrutable smile quirked the corners of his mouth.

'It's a pleasure to see you again, Denise after — how many years is it . . . ? Three! It seems a lifetime . . . Stand in the light, my dear, where I can see you.'

She hated herself because she found herself obeying him involuntarily. He had lost none of his hypnotic magnetism, which he used so ruthlessly on young women. Outwardly casual and suave, he was inwardly watching her like a fencer. He noted her clothes . . . fashionable dark dress under a mink coat . . . good shoes . . . expensive jewellery . . . So Denise was doing all right. Her make-up was heavy, but that haughty beauty was still there . . . She had the high cheekbones of an aristocrat, yet she had ascended from a London slum.

'I haven't come here to exchange compliments, Floyd,' she said. 'I want money — lots of it.'

He laughed bitterly. 'So do most of us, Denise — not excluding yours truly. As a matter of fact when I saw your glad rags I thought you might be good for a touch.'

'Don't bluff, Floyd. I've come here to demand what I'm entitled to.'

'And what's that?'

'Heart balm . . . You left me three years ago after you promised to marry me. You got out of it nicely, leaving the country when I needed you most.'

'You took me too seriously, Denise.' His eyes were lowered. He was coolly toying with a carved cigar box. 'Most women do.'

'Well, you can take me seriously now.'

He sighed. 'Of course, you know, you'll get no money out of me. Now stop acting the fool, Denise. The trick isn't coming off. You might as well keep cool. It's a pity you came all this way from town . . . Still, have a drink and some supper with me.'

For a full minute she struggled with her anger, realising she had to keep calm.

Then she said: 'The last time I had supper with you, I never saw you for three years.'

'And you won't see much of me after tonight, my dear. I won't allow you in my house again if you persist in taking that attitude.'

She matched her calmness with his.

'But I will see you all the same when I come down to collect my money. That will probably be every month.'

'What do you mean?' He was finished playing with the cigar box now. His jaw seemed ominous.

'I want a hundred pounds every month, with a first payment of five hundred, and that's letting you off cheaply.'

'Come on — out with it,' he said. 'What do you know?'

'Enough to get you hanged, darling. Remember the little Hazeltine girl?'

'You mean June Hazeltine?'

'Yes, she was murdered seven or eight months before you decided South Africa's climate suited you.'

'No? Really . . . ? Poor girl!'

'You murdered her, Floyd.'

His interrogative look held for a moment, and then dissolved into amusement.

'Don't be silly, Denise. I never murdered anyone in my life.'

'She's never been seen since a certain night in August and it's now exactly three-and-a-half years ago. I don't suppose many people know her last act was to visit your bungalow at Bracklehead.'

'These are serious accusations, Denise.'

'I was a blind fool when you left me to go to South Africa. I should have tackled you about it before you left, and I would if I'd known you did not intend to take me with you.' She sat on the arm of a velvet-covered chair and stared bitterly at the carpet. 'I've learnt a lot about June Hazeltine in the last three years,' she went on. 'And most of it was ghastly.'

'Been trying out your abilities as a detective, Denise?'

'Yes, I got in touch with the Breton sea-captain who took June's body out to sea and dropped it overboard. How did I get in touch? Well, I lived in your bungalow at Bracklehead for a month. I was curious. I thought I might find something, and I did. You'd sold the bungalow to some people who furnished it and let it to various other people. Well, I found a strange, old pipe stuffed up a chimney. Nothing much in that, but in Bracklehead harbour I saw a Breton sea-captain smoking an identical pipe. Odd, wasn't it?'

'So you got talking to him?' suggested Floyd Paget calmly.

'Yes. I showed him the pipe I'd found. He claimed it was his . . . The Breton was a huge lout. I got him drunk one night. We were very pally, Floyd. He told me he made these pipes for his own use. With the war being on, he'd been in Bracklehead a few years, so it wasn't surprising I found him. The Breton got boastful when he was drunk and he liked to tell me his adventures. He'd had plenty. I pretended to disbelieve him and he got wild, telling me some of his maddest exploits. He told me about taking a body from a bungalow at Bracklehead. He'd lost his pipe there. He'd had to make another.'

'A curious story,' commented Floyd Paget. He went to a sideboard and poured out a drink. He was about to drink the whisky when he seemed to remember the woman, and poured out another drink. He brought it to her.

'The police never suspected you as I did, Floyd. I guess June was just another missing girl case to them. If they'd stumbled on the Breton's pipe, they might have come to the same conclusions as I did. The Breton was quite a character at Bracklehead, and his boat was well-known. Why didn't you burn the pipe, Floyd?' She looked at him shrewdly: 'It was August, wasn't it? I suppose you'd have no fire going. So you stuffed the Breton's pipe up the chimney. You didn't want anything connecting the Breton with the bungalow. I guess June arrived secretly at the bungalow too. You'd see to that!'

Floyd Paget smiled broadly.

'Denise, this is an amazing story. Suppose — just suppose — you tried to prove it. I'm afraid you'd be laughed at.'

'Would you prefer me to go to the

police with the story? You're not fooling me, Floyd. I could easily prove how friendly you were with June Hazeltine; how you called for her at her theatre, and a few weekends you spent with her. I bet I could prove she was becoming an encumbrance like me and a few more women in your life. The police aren't fools, Floyd. One hint from me that June didn't just vanish, but was murdered, will bring the police down asking very awkward questions. You wouldn't like that, Floyd. You'd pay just to avoid answering those questions. You're going to pay, because I need money to live.'

'You're a clever cat!' he said throatily. 'Like all women!'

'I thought you loved the ladies!' she challenged. 'Don't tell me you've changed.'

He stamped round the room, his composure gone.

'Women! I've had nothing but trouble from women. Why won't they leave me alone?'

Watching him, she could have told him that the fault was within himself. Women figured as a procession in Floyd Paget's life and the termination of the affairs had featured many stormy episodes. Only Floyd Paget knew the truth of his affairs — and perhaps he had forgotten some in the last twenty-five years. He had never married. It was his boast that he was a fool with women, but never so foolish as that.

'Are you going to pay me the money?'

He dug his hands in his pocket and glowered.

Denise Hansen glanced at her watch. 'I want to get back to town. I've got someone to meet. What about it, Floyd? Are you going to force me to go to the police?'

He tried to touch her pity.

'Have you no feelings, Denise . . . ? I did mean something to you once . . . I am not so wealthy as you imagine, you know.'

His appeal fell on stony ground. 'Forget that stuff, Floyd.' She looked at her watch again. 'I'll want the money within two minutes.'

He pulled out a wallet, breathing deeply.

'I can manage only one hundred and

151

fifty. I don't carry a lot round with me.'

'I'll call again for the rest.' She stepped closer and took the notes. For a moment he had an insane desire to strangle her. He conquered the impulse. Better to make plans. Besides there was Hester ... yet another woman who probably knew too much.

He showed her to the door. He rather regretted that Davis, the butler, had seen Denise Hansen.

Denise climbed into her sports car. She felt a sense of grim satisfaction that she had brought off the first part of the game on such flimsy evidence. Of course, Floyd did not want the police asking questions. She let in the clutch, and the car swerved down the drive.

Floyd Paget went to his comfortable library to interview the young girl from whose presence he had begged to be excused while he talked to Denise Hansen. It was very probable that this second girl would be suitable for his purposes.

Hester Coyne rose as he entered the room.

'Sit down, my dear,' he said in that falsely-charming way of his.

Her youth and alertness attracted him like the moth to the candle or the alcoholic to old wine. She possessed more than prettiness; there was sheer beauty in her carriage, her grey eyes and dark hair. Hester had a certain youthful sophistication. Her face was candid, and she seemed intelligent. She was not an innocent fool.

She wore a full-length fur coat, but it was not expensive mink as Denise Hansen's was. Her gloves, shoes and hat were in faultless taste, yet they could be bought over the counter of the mass-production stores.

'I have a train to catch,' said Hester. 'I have been here two hours already and — '

'And I hope you will take the job, my dear Miss Coyne.'

She smiled readily.

'Well, I do need the job.'

'Then that's settled. I'll tell the housekeeper to prepare your room. A very good night, Miss Coyne.'

2

More Accusations

The second wayward woman came up the drive to Wilderhouse just as the evening dusk was settling over the huge pile of masonry next day. She stood looking round. She was small and she wore a sullen, determined expression, and her heavy shoes were planted firmly as she stood in the drive. She was wearing a tweed costume that gave her a stocky appearance, and yet there was some sulky fascination about the straight line of her mouth, her yellow hair and hard blue eyes.

A man left the main entrance of Wilderhouse and shambled down the drive towards her. It was Rory Thatcher, habitual thief and a recent recipient of His Majesty's hospitality — at Dartmoor. Rory had been trying to touch Paget for a couple of quid.

'Bloomin' toff, he is, miss,' Rory told the strange woman. 'If yer going to see Mister Paget, yer couldn't pick a better time. I've just had three whiskies with 'm. Yer can spin 'im any yarn. Haven't I seen you somewhere before, dearie?'

Her eyes flashed her disgust.

'No.'

She pushed past the man.

She was admitted to Wilderhouse and shown to Floyd Paget's library where she encountered Hester Coyne in a little outer room.

'Your name, please?' asked Hester pleasantly.

'Marian Smith.'

'To save time, just what experience have you to offer Mr. Paget? Do not be offended, but can you offer criticism of any particular prison that will be useful in the book he's writing?'

'I've never been in prison,' said Marian Smith.

'Well, Mr. Paget is building up a case against the administration of our prisons and wants to hear as many facts as possible.' Hester paused, and then said

155

patiently: 'What information have you to offer?'

'I haven't any. I want to see Mister Paget on a personal matter. I want to ask him how he'd like to be in prison himself!'

Hester was not startled. She noted Marian Smith's hard, sulky eyes. Hester had met a few queer people in the last three days — just as her employer had promised, and all their peculiarities had lessened her susceptibility to surprise. She had been very busy with a veritable stream of 'strange types'. She had taken down in shorthand stories of amazing abuse, incident and scorn of prison life. Already she had enough material to fill a large book, but some of the strange yarns would take a great deal of swallowing.

Writing down these accounts and meeting the yarn-spinners had, to a certain extent, put Hester's mind in a whirl. She believed Floyd Paget to be a zealous publicist with a bee in his bonnet. Yet somehow he didn't seem quite the type. He did not seem a bit like a crank. Neither in his dress, speech or habits was he cranky — in fact, he was quite charming.

Well, her job as secretary was fairly clear. If Mr. Paget wanted to interview hundreds of ex-convicts and other specimens of low strata that was his own affair.

'You'd better go in to see him,' Hester told Marian Smith doubtfully. Hester showed the other woman to the library door.

When the door had closed behind the woman, Hester sighed. The worst of working for a living was that you had to be so obedient to all sorts of people — especially the boss.

Hester sat down at her desk, which had been fixed in the small outer room, If Floyd Paget needed her, he would ring. Then, she supposed, she would have to concentrate upon getting down the woman's idiotic story. Hester sharpened her pencil and hummed to herself lightly and softly. She was an alert figure in her yellow blouse and grey skirt.

In the other room the newcomer, Marian Smith, gazed curiously at the man whose life was not an open book. He was sitting at a large desk, which was littered with papers. A mellow light diffused through the library, giving the rows of leather bound volumes a cosy appearance. The light emanates from two standard lamps, and a glowing fire added to the illumination.

Floyd Paget said: 'Please sit down.'

'So you don't remember me?'

'No.' He continued to smile, while his hand sought the butt end of the revolver that lay on a little ledge of the desk beside his knees. He did not know this woman. She was not the one he was seeking. But she looked dangerous. 'Ought I to know you . . . ? I've met so many people lately. I'm busy compiling information about our prisons. Are you here to help me or have you some other intention?'

'I have no intention of helping you.'

He gripped the revolver.

'Perhaps you'll tell me your exact intentions — why you have called? I'm sure they'd be interesting.'

She leaned closer.

'You are looking for Lena Spelb. You knew her three years ago, but you want to meet her badly now. You're hoping some of the lags who come here will tell you where she is. This campaign of yours is a lot of baloney. That girl you employ to type letters — she's part of the cover-up, isn't she? Or is she going the same way as my sister Bernadette?'

He did not shrink back, though there was fury in her face. He still smiled and gripped the revolver more firmly.

'I don't know anything about Bernadette.'

'Yes you do. She was a lovely kid . . . once. I'm her sister. I once saw you, and you should know me but I guess you've completely forgotten. You sent Bernadette to Lena Spelb. I think you had real money then and sending Bernadette to Madame Spelb was only an easy way out. But now you're looking for her because you want to make some easy money quick.'

'What do you want?' he said harshly.

'I would like to send you to eternal fire,' was the reply. 'But I'm only contacting you for the pleasure of letting you know you're up against me.'

He sneered in her face and raised his

revolver into view.

'I have a short way with people who threaten me.' He held the gun flat on the desk, pointing to her, and laughed.

Marian Smith was unafraid. The revolver might have been a toy for all the notice she took of it.

'Lena Spelb is in hiding,' she said. 'Oh, I know a great deal that may surprise you. Lena has changed her appearance a lot, too. I guess she'll understand when she hears about this stunt of yours. She'll be looking you up. She'll come along or one of her pals will contact you . . . I wonder why you want to go into Lena's racket? Are you hard up?'

He spoke very quietly.

'Get out of here. You're mad! I don't know what you want and I don't know anything about Bernadette. I've never heard of Lena Spelb either. Now get out!'

He stood up noisily. Marian Smith slid away from her seat towards the door. When she had gone, Paget beat down the fury inside him, and waited, not turning his head, but listening intently. He had heard a low, sharp scraping sound while pointing the revolver at Marian Smith. He knew the sound came from the french window. Someone was outside trying to open the window.

Suddenly he turned, walked swiftly to the window and jerked it open. It moved inwards. He held his revolver menacingly, and light from a nearby standard lamp glinted strongly on one side of the dull metal.

A man was outside the window. He was wearing a ginger overcoat and hat to match. He was a young man and he stepped into Floyd Paget's library with a confidence that figuratively swept aside the pointed gun. He was smiling. He had grey eyes in a healthy red face. He took out a cigarette and lit it quickly.

'Right across the deserts of Africa and the beaches of Normandy and the wide Rhine itself I've travelled,' he said cheerfully, 'and now I enter a gentleman's house at the point of a revolver. Got a permit for that toy Mr. Paget?'

'Who are you?'

'Edgar Cassidy, reporter for the *Daily Picture*. I thought I'd look you up.

There's a story in this reform book of yours.'

'Well, it would have been better if you'd come round by the front entrance,' said Paget gently. 'I'm sorry to point my gun at you.'

Edgar Cassidy waved his hand, dropping cigarette ash liberally. 'It's nothing. I've seen guns before. Anyway, you had a good reason to point it at the lady apparently.'

'She was beginning to be difficult. You will understand I have to protect myself against strange types.'

'Do you? Well, now for question and answer. Do you consider prison life a deterrent against repeated crime? I see you have a letter in the *Daily Projector* today.'

'Yes, I — '

'Nice place you've got here,' ran on the young man. 'Been shut up for a number of years, hasn't it? It's a wonder the government didn't move in and take it over.'

'I still have a little influence,' smiled Paget.

'Big place, too. Not much staff. I bet

plenty could happen in a large house like this. The walls are thick, and you can't hear the man in the next room.'

'Are you taking an inventory, young man?' asked Floyd smoothly.

'Yes,' said the young man disconcertingly. 'It's all part of my job.'

'Well, Mr. Cassidy, for your benefit nothing very exciting does happen here, even if the walls are very thick.'

'That dame you had to point a gun at — who was she? What was the matter with her?' Edgar Cassidy's honest red face and ginger coat and hat gave him the appearance of a young farmer. Nothing indicated that under the ginger hat there was a brain that could dart like lightning to the core of a story.

'I think she was unbalanced,' said Paget with a smile.

'Well, send us a letter tomorrow and we might print it,' said young Mr. Cassidy. He grabbed the door handle and left the room before Paget could point out he might as well depart the way he had arrived.

Edgar Cassidy stared down at Hester Coyne in the small outer room. Here the light was stronger, but Edgar didn't need strong light to look at Hester.

'Right across the deserts of Africa to the beaches of Normandy and across the wide Rhine itself,' murmured Edgar. 'And what do I find? A sweet lady in the house of the monster.'

Hester looked up, startled.

'Where did you come from?'

'I've just told you. From the beaches of Normandy — '

'Down that passage and turn to the right,' she said severely. 'That's the way out.'

'What makes you work here?' demanded Edgar Cassidy, unabashed

'I'm Mr. Paget's secretary. Now please go down that passage and — '

'Is there a village nearby?'

'No, of course not. Wilderhouse stands alone.'

'And you live in this house?'

'Yes. I have a room. There are servants and — '

Edgar sat on the corner of the table that served as her desk and he removed his hat.

'I don't like it,' he said. 'I don't like

'your being here.'

'And I don't like ex-crooks telling me their preferences,' she said furiously

'The name is Edgar Cassidy, reporter for the *Daily Picture*,' he said calmly. 'If there'd been a village nearby, I'd have stayed at the local pub and if you'd got into trouble you could have 'phoned me to help you.'

'Good heavens, why should I get into trouble?'

'Lady, there's always trouble wherever I go,' the reporter said seriously. 'Perhaps it's because I can smell trouble a week ahead. Perhaps it's because I'm born that way. But as soon as I approach anything, trouble pops up ahead of me and I blunder into it. But it's all right with me so long as there's a story in it.'

'Well, you needn't worry about me, Mr. Cassidy,' she said coolly. 'I'm not in trouble,'

She rattled the space bar of her typewriter. Behind her the library door opened and Floyd Paget came out.

'I will send your paper a letter in the morning, Mr. Cassidy. I'm very earnest about these reform measures.'

Edgar put his ginger hat back on his head.

'That's great, Reforms are topical. Incidentally, I'm getting a new angle on the subject — your secretary's viewpoint on the campaign. That should be more interesting than yours.'

Paget stalked out of the room.

When he had gone, Edgar turned to the girl and said sadly:

'Honey, don't you know you're working for a man whose reputation with women smells like a dozen bad eggs?'

She stood up and so was able to look down at him as he sat on a corner of the table.

'I've heard nothing about that,' she said coldly. 'And I don't believe it. Mr. Paget has always been considerate to me.'

He grinned at her amiably and shifted off the table. 'He's playing for time, precious — '

The door of the little room opened and Paget came in again.

'There will be no more work for today, Miss Coyne,' Paget said. 'I should think you'd like to go to your room and rest. We may have a heavy day tomorrow.'

'Thank you, Mr. Paget. I think I will go to my room.'

Her employer withdrew. Edgar Cassidy shook his head wearily.

'Why don't you come with me?' he said. 'I've got a car waiting. We could find an inn somewhere. We've got lots to talk about.'

'Sorry, Mr. Cassidy. I'm not interested.'

She showed him the way out of Wilderhouse. He stood in the vast hall and memorised the position of the staircase and the doors leading off. Then he went out into the night, remembering every word of the conversation between Floyd Paget and Marian Smith — though he did not know the woman's name. By pressing his ear against the glass french window he had heard a surprising amount.

In a ground floor sitting room Floyd Paget still waited for the third wayward woman — Lena Spelb by name — a woman more evil than Wilderhouse itself.

3

Edgar Intervenes

Edgar Cassidy stood in the dark grounds round Wilderhouse and watched the lights in the windows. There was not a big display of illumination, but he discovered Hester Coyne's room on the first floor. He even saw the girl come to the window and pull the red curtains across the panes. Edgar drew hard on his cigarette. There was something desirable about Hester Coyne. It was not just her figure, her face or her hands. Ninety-nine million other women had the same things, but only an odd few like Cleopatra or Betty Grable could make anything out of them. Hester Coyne was one of the odd few.

Edgar wondered about Floyd Paget. Before coming down to Wilderhouse he had gleaned many facts from a woman gossip-writer he knew and the picture of the ageing roué as an author-reformer did not add up. He'd known then there was a story somewhere.

Edgar walked along a narrow path, blundered into a flowerbed and cursed the damp soil that clung to his shoes. A second later he froze behind a tree, watching the drive. A car crawled up like a black slug with gleaming eyes. It halted, pouring white light on the flight of wide stairs leading to the entrance of Wilder-house.

A woman got out. She was a black figure, and before leaving the car she turned the headlights to dim. Edgar saw her walk before the dim lights as she mounted the stairs. She was tall, taller than himself, and she had shoulders like a man. She was wearing a long, black fur coat. He could not see her face.

She was admitted to Wilderhouse by the butler. The door closed upon the woman, and Edgar extracted his shoes from the sticky soil. He cursed again. He did not like brown shoes covered with soil. He was rather particular about his shoes.

He walked towards the woman's car,

making sure that the woman had not left a companion in the car. But the vehicle was empty and he opened the door, glanced round the interior quickly. There was nothing lying around. The car might have just left a showroom, such was its condition. He dived his hand into the door pockets, but they were empty.

He left the car quickly. He was in time to see two figures move across the lighted window of a ground floor room, then heavy curtains were drawn. But Edgar had seen Paget and his woman visitor.

Edgar stood in the shelter of two huge bushes, considering. Should he beat it to his car?

His cogitations were cut by glimpsing a fleeting figure. The figure darted from the thick shrubbery surrounding Wilderhouse and made for a dark ground-floor window. The figure wrestled with the window for a few seconds and then succeeded in pushing up the frame. In another second the figure vanished into the dark room.

'I'll swear that's yet another woman,' murmured Edgar. 'How many of them are running around this nut-house?'

He moved towards the window, found it opened easily and he climbed through muttering: 'I guess it's visiting night.'

He had to feel his way through a dark room filled with large pieces of furniture. The woman who had entered before him had vanished.

He walked across the hall in silence, hands in his ginger overcoat. He stopped once to wipe the soil from his shoes on to a big mat near the entrance. Then he went over to the recess which gave to a door which he guessed would open to the room wherein Floyd Paget and his woman visitor were talking.

He hadn't any idea where the unknown intruder had gone to. He stopped beside the door, listening. He could not hear the slightest sound. He looked round. Behind him was another door. He did not bother to open the door because there came to his ears the quick steps of a woman. Someone was walking across the hall.

Edgar peered round the edge of the wall making the recess. He saw Hester Coyne walking quickly across the floor.

He stepped out and said: 'Hello.'

She turned in surprise.

'Good heavens, haven't you gone yet?'

'I did go, but I saw a woman enter by a window so I followed her. I saw another woman who was admitted as if she was a lady. I don't know if she was one or not. Say, a lot of women come and go in this morgue of a house.'

'Well, you'd better leave,' said Hester indignantly. 'You seem a little mad. I don't believe you saw a woman enter by a window, I think you're concocting a yarn.'

He smiled humourously.

'I thought you were bidden to stay in your room, weren't you?'

'I left my cigarettes on my desk — and I'm not bidden to do anything!'

'Who is the lady Paget is entertaining?' he asked.

'My dear Mr. Cassidy, I haven't the slightest idea.'

'Come here,' he said abruptly. He caught her hand and led the surprised girl to the door of the room in which Paget and the third wayward woman were cloistered. 'Hear anything?' he asked.

They were near to the thick door. 'Maybe you'll recognise the lady's voice. Maybe she's been here before and if she was, I'd like to know something about her.'

But the low conversation of two persons in a large room cannot travel through a thick oak door. The construction of Wilderhouse was on a massive scale. The builders had evidently considered walls valueless unless totally soundproof.

'I wish you'd let go my hand,' said Hester impatiently.

Edgar reluctantly relaxed his grasp.

The next instant all the lights went out. The hall and the recess were plunged into impenetrable darkness. Hester gasped. Edgar said: 'Not my doing, I assure you.' He struck a match and while it was flaring, he saw the handle of the door before him move.

He heard the rattle as someone on the other side made to open the door. Edgar leaped back, remembering the door immediately behind him. He twisted the knob, wrenched the door open and grabbed Hester.

'In here,' he said. 'It's dangerous to be

caught spying, y'know.'

He pushed her forward. She was surprised at his strength and, in the confusion of the moment, did not resist. Edgar bundled in after her, drawing the door quickly behind him. It was all the work of a few seconds. Edgar calculated Paget would find the recess empty when he opened his sitting room door.

But in another second Edgar cursed inwardly. He and Hester were in a tiny cloak-cupboard. He had not expected the door to lead to such a diminutive space as this. The cupboard had not the depth of an average wardrobe.

'You're nearly pressing the life out of me!' gasped Hester. 'Have a heart!'

He could feel her close to him. Her body was something real, and he could smell the perfume of her hair. He did not know what to do with his hands. If he held them straight down they were touching her skirt. He tried raising them. His hands were now close to her bare arms. He could feel the smoothness of her skin. He had to hang on to something otherwise he would fall against her with all his weight. He steadied himself by grasping her shoulders.

'You're a nuisance!' said Hester tensely. 'Why did you have to rush in here?'

'Your boss is a queer bird up to some queer game,' he said hoarsely. 'He was coming out of the room into the passage recess. If he once thought you were spying on him, your life would be a little unpleasant.'

'But I could explain without hiding in this ridiculous manner.'

There was a deep silence. He could feel the rise and fall of her body as she tried to strain away from him. Edgar cursed again. It looked as if he was spoiling things for himself. Then he heard sounds in the passage outside.

Paget was complaining about the lights, and then there was a slow metallic voice that could only belong to Floyd Paget's lady visitor. Edgar had never heard a more sinister voice belonging to a woman. It was a voice that seemed to be soaked in sophistication.

Edgar wished they would get the lights on again and retire to their confab. His face was only inches from the girl's. Gradually her white face showed in relief to the utter blackness. All the time he was conscious of an electric atmosphere — of her unspoken suspicion of him.

Then a shot rang out.

Hester started and instinctively her hands clutched him. They heard the clatter of footsteps outside in the recess and then a scream.

It was a woman's scream of pure terror. Edgar guessed it came from the ground floor opposite the cupboard.

'Let's get out of this!' he grunted.

He pushed on the cupboard door and they tumbled out into the recess. At the same time the lights went on again, illuminating the big circular hall and the recess.

Inside the sitting room it seemed hell was breaking loose. A woman was screaming like a mad thing. Edgar flung the half-open door wide open. He lurched into the room, and his hands were not in his overcoat pockets.

He saw the woman who, an hour earlier, had sat in front of Paget while he pointed a revolver. Marian Smith was struggling with the tall woman in the black fur coat. The tall woman was busy playing with Marian Smith like a cat plays with a mouse. She seemed to have enormous strength — as much if not more than an athletic man. This freakish, masculine strength was evident upon her face. Lena Spelb had a grotesque, mannish face. There was a savage, jeering expression upon her long face and the twisted lips, red with lipstick, seemed a mockery of all that was feminine.

Edgar flung himself forward. He saw the gun lying on the ground and he darted for it. He guessed the gun had just recently fired the shot they'd heard while in the cupboard. Instinctively he knew that the woman now screaming had used the revolver. He wondered who she'd tried to shoot. It seemed that it was she who had entered Wilderhouse by the window. Had she tampered with the lights, too?

He grabbed the gun.

'Stand back!' he rapped. He planted himself before the grotesque tall woman, at the same time quickly satisfying himself that the revolver magazine was loaded. Lena Spelb fell back, releasing Marian Smith. The smaller, yellow-haired woman groaned and staggered towards Edgar.

'Keep her off me! She's a fiend!'

Hester approached in amazement, her throat suddenly parched. She caught Marian Smith, held her shoulders and tried to comfort her.

'Get me out of here! That's Lena Spelb — the woman who sold my sister Bernadette! She's not human. I wished I'd killed her when I fired. She's not a woman — she's a beast!'

Suddenly Hester saw the whole edifice of respectability, which she believed belonged to Floyd Paget, fall to the ground.

There was no doubt of the evil etched in Lena Spelb's repellent face, She glared at Marian Smith malevolently.

'Take that mad woman away,' she said. Her voice was like a harsh metallic recording. 'She tried to shoot me. She's been fooling with the lights.'

At that moment Paget returned. He

stared round the scene in his sitting room.

'So it is the mad Miss Smith who is creating all the disturbance! I have just replaced a fuse, which you apparently pulled out. And, Mr. Cassidy, I see you are on the scene as usual.'

'All the way from the deserts of Africa — ' began Edgar.

'May I ask how you came to be in this house?'

'I heard a shriek,' said Edgar melodramatically, 'and so I rushed in.'

'I'd be obliged if you'd leave the grounds of Wilderhouse. Your newspaper must surely be lost without you.'

'Yes, I'm going,' declared Edgar. 'And I'm taking two ladies with me — Miss Coyne and Miss Smith.'

'Indeed! Miss Coyne happens to be my secretary and as for Miss Smith, I shall have the pleasure of handing her over to the police for a murderous attack on my guest.'

Edgar grinned disbelievingly.

'You wouldn't go near the police. And Lena Spelb hates their guts. The police and a few others hate her ugly dial, too.

No sir, I'm taking your secretary and Marian Smith into safety.'

Paget twisted his full lips.

'Hester, this young man is out of his senses. I hope you'll stay on here at your job. I need you. I'm most sorry about this alarming disturbance but how can I prevent a mad woman who threatens me and later enters the house, removes a fuse and tries to shoot my guest?'

But Hester, her intuition working strongly, looked at the guest and felt a shudder run down her spine. She could not subdue her newfound suspicions of Floyd Paget.

'I'm taking Marian Smith to the office,' stated Edgar. His grey eyes were pugnacious. 'There's a story somewhere . . . Hester, go to your room and pack your bag. You can't stay in the house of this beast.'

To emphasize his words, Edgar pointed the revolver at Paget and Lena Spelb.

Hester nearly told Edgar she didn't like the way he gave orders but she hesitated. Actually, she didn't fancy staying another night at Wilderhouse. Things were happening that had no relation to Mr. Paget's prison reform campaign; and if the horrible caricature of a woman known as Lena Spelb was staying the night in Wilderhouse, then she, Hester, was going

Edgar and the two girls backed out of the room. Paget and Lena Spelb stood watching like theatrical figures.

Edgar and Marian Smith followed Hester up the staircase.

'I can lend you a jumper,' said Hester, and she put an arm round the other woman. They mounted the stairs, and Edgar threw glances backwards. He was not quite sure of the reaction of the man and woman downstairs. He was not sure of a few things. He'd heard Marian Smith's story through the french window, but maybe the woman was distorting things, though he didn't think she was distorting them much.

Lena Spelb was glaring at Paget.

'Fine plans you're making! Who is that mad woman? I don't know her. What was she saying about her sister?'

He stamped impatiently towards the glowing fireplace.

'She called here earlier . . . threatening

me . . . You disposed of her sister for me years ago . . . She remembers and apparently knows you . . . Evidently the woman hung around the grounds . . . '

Silently they walked along an unlighted passage, and passed Hester's room from which voices could be heard. Paget showed Lena into an adjacent bedroom. He said: 'I've an interesting mechanism in here. I used it once on a fool blonde who proved rather difficult. It's a novel kind of gas chamber in the guise of a bedroom.'

4

The Body in the Car

Edgar went into the bedroom with Hester and Marian Smith. The smaller woman was now sullen and, with her torn clothes and yellow hair, she looked like some peasant woman who had been thrashed.

Edgar looked round the room and held the revolver loosely.

'What's your story?' he asked. 'Why the devil did you try to shoot Lena Spelb? Give it me brief.'

'I wanted to shoot Paget,' Marian told them. 'I hung around until it was really dark, working up my nerve. Then I saw Lena Spelb arrive, and I knew then I'd kill both of them. A few years ago Paget got rid of my sister Bernadette through Lena Spelb. How do I know? Because I made enquiries. I even lived in one of Lena's dives.' Marian Smith stared defiantly. 'I don't care about anything. I only cared about getting even with Paget and that horrible woman.'

Edgar turned. He was tired of staring at a blank wall. He wanted to look at Hester again. He found Marian Smith struggling into a scarlet jumper. He turned his gaze and Edgar watched Hester packing her large suitcase.

'Well, I'm the giddy rescuer after all.'

Hester said coldly: 'Perhaps it's a case of the frying pan to the fire. How do I know I can trust you?'

He felt suddenly weary.

'You don't know anything,' he groaned. 'And neither do I, except that Paget fellow downstairs is a perfect swine with women and he's plotting some scheme with Lena Spelb. Lena is Mistress of the Horrible, so you can make a good guess at the scheme and maybe Marian can help you in your conclusions. Come on; let's get out of here and throw bricks at Paget from a safe distance. You were pretty silly to take a job like this — miles from anyone and in the same house as that roué.'

'I — I thought it was a great chance to

make good . . . I needed a job. Now I'm wondering if I can claim any salary.'

'When the police get Paget you can write me a story entitled: 'I was Secretary to the Beast'. Then you'll cash in.'

'I'm ready to go,' said Marian Smith. She added: 'But I'm not finished with Paget and Lena Spelb.'

'If you've any sense, you'll give the police your story and then put the whole thing out of your mind,' advised Edgar Cassidy.

'Like blazes I will. This is personal. I don't like the police.'

Edgar could not explain his increasing weariness until suddenly the sweet odour in the air became pungent and his eyes felt like lead flaps. Previously he had ascribed the faint, sweet smell to some perfume the two girls carried but now, as he swam painfully out of some nightmarish weariness, he knew better.

He walked with swaying steps to the door. The three or four yards seemed endless and the floor was like a billowing cloud. He collided with Hester, who was standing with her hands to her eyes, swaying. Everything was swaying and tremulous, like figures seen through a heat haze.

He grasped the door handle and moved it slowly. The door seemed immovable. He lurched clumsily with, his full weight, jerking the handle and trying to pull the door inwards.

He felt like a child in his helplessness. A thump sounded behind him, coming to his deadened mind like something unexplainable. He turned sickeningly. Mistily he saw Hester lying on the floor.

He swayed over to her, his legs threatening to buckle up. He clutched at the bed and drew himself to Hester as she lay on a rug, apparently drugged.

Grimacing horribly in an effort to force his brain and eyes to function, he pulled out his handkerchief and stumbled over to a small table beside the bed. He could see a glass of water. He knew it was a glass of water even if the thing seemed to circle sickeningly. He reached out for the glass with a lifeless arm. He tried to dip his handkerchief in the glass — and then he was aware that the glass was lying on its side.

Savagely he made his brain work. He jabbed at his brain with some willpower culled from heaven knows where, and his brain directed his numb hand to dab his handkerchief in the pool of water on the little table.

Then Edgar fell down beside the table. He curled like a fatally-injured insect and lay still. He could feel the sweet, drugged air soothing out all his harsh worries. It was easy to sleep . . . fatally easy.

But Edgar Cassidy was a man in whom the human will to fight burned strongly. With a sudden effort he flexed all his muscles and gripped the sodden handkerchief bringing it close to his nose and mouth. Then he curled again. In his mind was a dim plan. It was hardly a plan but rather an instinct. He curled, handkerchief to his nose, breathing with difficulty through the soaked cloth. All the time he had to fight his senseless desire to slip into the abyss. He lay waiting for his enemies — a half-drugged man with a stubborn will to fight.

Paget, in the next room with Lena Spelb, turned off the master-tap and shut the cupboard door, hiding the gas cylinders.

'Well, you've got yourself two pretties,' he remarked to Lena. 'As for the man, I'll dump him somewhere. If it were necessary, I wouldn't hesitate to kill him, but he has no real evidence against us and I shall take care that he never gets any. Here, take this respirator.'

They fitted the mask-like respirators over their noses and mouths and went into the passage. Paget turned the key of Hester's room and then put it into his pocket. He had always found it useful to have keys to his employees' rooms.

He went straight to the window and opened it. The sweet gas went surging out into the night air. Lena was staring down at the two prone girls. This tall, mannish, travesty of a woman appeared to be gloating.

Paget stared at Hester grimly and broodingly. The girl had haunted him from the moment he'd first met her. Her freshness and indefinable air of breeding had impressed him. All the time he'd known he'd wanted to master her.

'They'll be unconscious for at least an hour,' he said.

'That gives us time to get them to my place,' said Lena Spelb throatily through the respirator.

She poked at Edgar's prone body with her foot.

'A pity I can't use this fool, too.'

Suddenly the 'fool' sat up, one hand holding a damp handkerchief and the other a revolver. Edgar swayed, fighting a desire to vomit and slide into the black depths of the drug that dragged at him. He was sweating. He felt ghastly. He wished he were in bed with Hester tending him and not having to fight, fight, fight . . .

He dared not stand. He sat swaying, but the revolver pointed at the two persons whose eyes above their respirators betrayed their surprise. Edgar had forgotten the revolver when the dopey gas had first affected him. He had forgotten everything in his effort to crawl out of a mile-deep black chasm.

'Open that door, Paget,' said Edgar thickly, 'or I'll plug you in the guts where it'll hurt most.'

The other slowly opened the door.

'Get away from me, Lena,' said Edgar. 'Over beside Paget.'

She took mannish strides towards her companion.

Edgar got up like a boxer who is nearly counted out.

He staggered over to the door and gradually backed out with the all-important weapon menacing Lena and Paget. In the open doorway the air was cleaner and Edgar threw away his damp handkerchief and gulped lungfuls of air.

The two people inside the room watched him like wary animals. So far it was checkmate, but if he slipped up they'd be on to him. How the devil was he to get Hester and the other girl out of the room single-handed? He beckoned to Lena and Paget.

'Come on out. Don't think I'm worried about shooting. I once shot Nazis for the fun of it. Come out. You're going into another room.'

That was the idea: to lock them in another room while he got Hester and Marian Smith out of Wilderhouse to his car.

Paget and Lena Spelb came towards him, removing their respirators. Edgar edged away from them to a safe distance.

'Go along the passage,' he ordered.

His mind was working better now, though he still felt as though he'd drank neat chloroform, and he guessed that the drug gas had issued from a nearby room, so it was no use pushing the two captives into an adjacent room.

They came to a spot where the passage led to a staircase. Edgar switched on lights and noticed a likely room.

'In there,' he ordered.

He was still puzzled about what to do with his captives. They went into the room and Edgar noticed it was empty, but in one corner was a cupboard with a door that had a catch that could only be opened from the outside.

'I had to hide in a cupboard, myself,' bantered Edgar. 'With a girl, too. It wasn't so good as you'd think. Well, you can jam yourself in there with Lena. You'll be in good company.'

Paget opened the cupboard door. The interior seemed a lot larger than the place in which Edgar had hidden with Hester.

'In here?' inquired Paget mockingly.

'Yes. It'll keep you safe until I get the two girls off the premises.'

With exaggerated courtesy, Paget allowed Lena Spelb to enter first. When the tall woman had disappeared, the man followed. Grimly Edgar came closer and shut the door. He gave it a few shoves to make sure the catch was holding. Then he ran back along the passage and entered Hester's room.

The two girls were lying as he had left them. The drug had bowled them over completely, and he had no idea when they would recover. It might be an hour or it might be two. In any case he could not wait until they recovered their senses. He intended to carry them out to his car.

Edgar had to make a choice, and he had no hesitation in taking Hester first. He put her over his shoulder and, gun in hand, ran out of the room and down the staircase. He made a strange figure as he cut across the big hall to the entrance. Wilderhouse seemed a curiously silent house

In the drive he passed Lena Spelb's car and wondered if he should smash something. He ran on without stopping. All he had to do was collect Marian Smith, and then Paget and Lena Spelb would be just another headline

He found his car in the leafy lane where he had left it. He placed Hester in the rear seat and looked closely at her to see if she showed any sign of returning life. But she was still in a deep slumber.

He tore back and turned into the Wilderhouse drive. No one saw him rush up the drive and through the open entrance doors. He gripped the revolver, more as a precaution than anything else, as he took the stairs two at a time. He came to Hester's room and remembered that he had forgotten her suitcase. If he meant to get it, he would have to carry that as well as Marian Smith. He cursed. He found some consolation in the fact that Paget was closeted with the unpleasant Lena Spelb.

Then, as he looked round the room, he realised that something had gone wrong. Marian Smith was not in sight. He wrenched open a wardrobe. Empty! Thinking the strong-willed girl might have recovered her senses he dashed across the passage to the open bathroom door. The bathroom was deserted.

What did it mean? Had Marian Smith got up and walked away or had Paget and Lena escaped?

Edgar did not know. He did know, however, that if Floyd Paget and Lena were free, Hester was in danger. She was lying defenceless in the car. He ran downstairs two at a time, whole-heartedly cursing Wilderhouse and all its inhabitants. Taking Hester's bag with him did not exactly add to his speed, but he hung on to it all the same. He saw the familiar form of his modest saloon car in the gloom and he ended his sprint in a leap.

He wrenched open the car door. He put out a hand to grip Hester's shoulder. Her head lolled on her shoulder. Apparently she was still unconscious. It was gloomy in the lane. Edgar drew back to switch on a light inside the car when he suddenly realised the state of his hands.

They were red with blood.

He did not need light to tell him it was blood. He could smell the warm, sticky fluid. The horror of it momentarily stunned him. Hardened as he was to crime, this ghastly act made him shudder.

Hester! The swines had killed Hester! Red rage made Edgar clench his sticky hands. The blood squeezed through his fingers, and he felt revolted.

He groped blindly for the switch inside the car. He would have to see if something could be done for Hester, but it was unlikely that the inhuman swine had blundered.

The thin yellow light jerked on. Edgar turned to the body of the girl.

He received another shock that whirled his brain into deep relief.

The girl in the rear seat was not Hester. It was Marian Smith!

That she was dead, there was no doubt. A pool of blood had collected on the leather seat and was dripping down to the floorboards. Into Edgar's mind flashed another question.

Where was Hester?

She might be sharing the fate of

Marian Smith. Someone had followed him down to the car — probably taking Marian Smith along at the same time — and removed the unconscious Hester some minutes after he had left her.

Undoubtedly this was the work of Floyd Paget or Lena Spelb. For some reason they had murdered Marian Smith and deposited the body in his car.

Why the blazes should they do such a damn-fool thing?

Perhaps if a village cop came cycling along just now, things would look bad. 'Motorist Found With Body of Dead Girl in His Car'. Edgar saw it in headlines. It didn't look so good, even if he could explain his way out.

He gave the dead girl another glance. She had been stabbed, judging by the blood, but there was no sign of a weapon. That was something in his favour. If this crime was being pinned on him, someone would have to find a weapon and prove he'd handled it.

Edgar wiped his hands on an oily duster, which he kept in the car. He walked away from the car and came to a position where he could see Wilderhouse. He wondered if Hester was still in the old house. He wondered if she were still alive. Then he remembered he had a revolver. What the blazes was he waiting for?

He'd have to be careful. Lena Spelb and Floyd Paget had obviously got out of that cupboard. No one else could have murdered Marian Smith. Lena and the man who wanted to cash in on her racket might be waiting for him. They'd be fools if they weren't.

That was it. They would expect him to come back. If he burst in like some movie hero, he'd probably get a tap on the head or perhaps his guts full of lead, and a kick in the face to help him on his way.

Edgar came up the drive once more, walking slowly and grimly. He saw the car standing before the flight of stairs leading to Wilderhouse's front entrance. He thought it was Lena Spelb's until he realised Lena's car had been all black and this one was a dinky little model in grey.

Now who the devil did the car belong to? And for that matter, where was Lena Spelb's car?

He came round the little grey sports car just as someone climbed out. He held his gun straight.

A woman in a mink coat stood on the drive. She turned her head suddenly and saw Edgar. She started involuntarily at the sight of the gun. Edgar came grimly towards her. It seemed he was fated to act like a gangster, but he wanted to ask questions and get true answers.

5

The Inhuman Figure

The woman in the mink coat flattened against her car door.

'Who are you?' she gasped.

'I'm going to ask the same question,' retorted Edgar.

'I'm Denise Hansen.'

'Well, Denise, I reckon you know who lives here. What do you want with him? Cut it short because I've got lots to do.'

'I'm here to see Floyd Paget. If this is a hold-up, you've got the wrong person.' The woman gave a bitter laugh. 'I'm the one who is continually hard-up.'

'It isn't a hold-up. But there's going to be fireworks inside Wilderhouse in a few minutes, so I advise you to steer clear. Go for a run in your car. Call again in the morning. Maybe you'll see Paget and maybe you won't. He might be stiff, and rather nasty to look at.'

'What do you mean?'

'Get into your car and back out,' ordered Edgar impatiently. 'I tell you this is no time to visit Paget. Now get going!'

'You're going to kill him!'

'Get going, I say.'

'If you're going to kill him,' said the woman coolly, 'you might let me come along. I hate him. I hate everything he does. I'll help you to kill him, if you like.'

Edgar narrowed his eyes. He was beginning to think Wilderhouse a rendezvous for criminal lunatics.

'Why do you want to kill Paget?' he rapped.

Denise Hansen had the shrewdest wits in London. She was using them now. She stared through the gloom at this medium-sized man in a thick overcoat and small hat.

'He's stopped some money I'm accustomed to getting from him,' she said rapidly. 'I've got a murder charge hanging over him, but he's too clever so he's stopped my hush money. I think he's found a way out of the evidence I've got against him.'

'You were blackmailing him, huh?'

'Call it what you like,' she snapped. 'He murdered a girl I used to know. That was three years ago, but I've been waiting all the time he was in South Africa. I've got real scores against him. He's a dirty waster.'

'Do you know that Lena Spelb, the woman who runs night clubs, is in the house or has just left?' asked Edgar.

'Lena! She gives me the creeps. I once saw her at Ralvini's. She's supposed to be lying low, so I'm told. What does Paget want with her?'

'They've just murdered a girl and kidnapped another,' said Edgar. He added: 'They've kidnapped the girl I want to marry.'

Because he saw no reason why not, he gave Denise Hansen the story briefly.

'I'm going into the house now,' he ended. 'I've wasted too much time talking already. I advise you to beat it.'

He moved off, and then half-turned to see if she took his advice. She was running after him. She clutched his arm.

'I'm coming with you. I hate that guy, I tell you.'

'I've never heard of you,' said Edgar

seriously. 'I don't know how you fit in. Now beat it, kid.'

'You say you want to get a girl away from Paget. Well, I could help you,' Denise insisted. 'How are you going to stick up two people and get an unconscious girl away? Let me come with you.'

There was something in her argument and Edgar realised that two were better than one. He gave in.

'For mercy's sake, let's get cracking. I want to find out what's happened to Hester.'

He went straight to the front entrance. He was surprised and wary to find it opened to his pressure. He slipped into the hall and then stood staring around. Only one light was giving illumination and the place was full of shadows. Wilderhouse seemed to be empty. No servant appeared to inquire their business. Edgar concluded Paget gave his servants specific orders to stay below.

Edgar turned and saw that Denise Hansen had followed him. He crept along to the recess just off the hall and grasped the door handle of the sitting room. He jerked it open suddenly and stepped to one side. He looked into the room. The light was out, but red flickering shapes sprang from a good fire.

A figure reclining on a large easy chair attracted his attention. He looked closer. The figure was that of a man dressed in light-coloured suit. Edgar frowned. He was sure Paget had worn a dark lounge suit.

'Come in, Mr. Cassidy,' said a voice.

Edgar strolled grimly through the doorway and stopped. He cocked his gun at the reclining figure. The man seemed very composed. A flame from the fire leaped and Edgar saw Paget's features with his dark greyish hair and full lips. Paget might have been wrapt in meditation. He was quite motionless and seemed to be staring into the fire fixedly.

Edgar said: 'Where's Hester?'

'My dear Cassidy, she's gone with Lena Spelb. Didn't you see her car leave?' Paget's voice was full of satisfaction. But the figure did not move.

'You murdered Marian Smith!' Edgar barked.

'Yes, and Lena and I got out of the cupboard quite simply because it has a door leading into the other room. We could have caught you taking Hester away, but I didn't like to challenge you with that gun in your hand. We knew we could trick you. Marian Smith is almost as strong-willed as yourself, Cassidy. She recovered her senses a little when we moved her. She tried to fight and then Lena stabbed her. Lena is a hellcat. It was Lena's idea of a joke to plant the body in your car. You'd better go back to your newspaper and think out some harmless story, Cassidy. You've lost Hester.'

Edgar sensed truth in the words. He felt a wild fury grip him. He raised his revolver, aiming at the chest of the reclining figure. He felt an overpowering urge to shoot him dead. But at the last second, he controlled his murder-lust and lowered the barrel, aiming deliberately at Paget's legs. He fired point-blank three times and, amid the echoes of the shot, he heard Denise Hansen shriek piercingly. Even as he pumped the shots into the figure, he wondered what manner of madness prompted the man to sit so motionless and offer a target.

Denise Hansen screamed like a maniac and groped for the light switch. Edgar stared unbelievingly at the man he'd shot. Three shots had ripped their way into their target. Any human man would have squirmed in absolute agony. Edgar wondered if he was going mad.

The figure had hardly moved. Paget continued to sit and smile into the fire. It was an inhuman performance. Paget spoke again.

'You are not very clever, Cassidy!'

Edgar croaked and began to doubt his senses. He stepped backwards and trod heavily on Denise Hansen's foot. The next instant the light went on flooding the whole room with brilliant light. The glaring illumination swept all Edgar's hideously-jumbled thoughts into ordered sequence. One glance and the truth of the reclining figure was revealed.

It was a figure all right. A waxwork dummy! It was Paget's life-size dummy and its transfixed smile was undisturbed by three bullets. The set-up meant a trap. It would be an amusing trap to Paget. The man was hiding somewhere because a waxwork dummy cannot speak. With these thoughts revolving in his brain, Edgar tried to back out of the room. He turned and blundered into a wildcat woman — Denise.

'You swine!' she yelled. 'I'm not with you! If you kill Paget you stop all my chances of getting money from him. I was lying to you, you fool, because I thought I could trick you!'

Edgar roughly pushed Denise to one side with his arm. He had to get out.

Lena Spelb had Hester. He did not doubt that Paget was speaking the truth.

The man had enjoyed the mockery.

Meanwhile. Denise Hansen clawed at Edgar, and her screams sounded in his ears like a siren. He stamped from the door into the recess dragging Denise Hansen with him. He stopped to hammer her wrists free from him while she shrieked: 'Floyd — Floyd Paget!'

If the commotion didn't waken the servants, then they certainly had been given extraordinary instructions, thought Edgar bitterly. It was his last thought before something crashed on his head with a ghastly shooting pain that tailed into a myriad coloured lights and finally a deep, black pit.

Paget stepped round the sharp, concealing corner that made the recess and placed his revolver in his pocket as Edgar slumped to the floor.

'I wish you'd stop your damned commotion!' snapped Paget.

Denise Hansen leaned against a wall and tried to subdue her hysterical noises.

'He was coming to kill you, Floyd. I thought I'd trick him . . . So I pretended to agree with him . . . I was waiting my chance . . . '

'Why the blazes are you here?'

'I need money. More money. I've had some bad luck. But we can talk about that later, Floyd. What are you going to do with this snooper?'

'I'll have to ditch the fool somewhere.'

'You could kill him. What does he know about you?'

'He thinks he knows quite a lot, but he could not prove anything. Where is the proof? It is only his word against mine — except that Lena Spelb stabbed a girl,'

His eyes glinted. 'That will need attention. She's a dangerous woman! I told her it was risky leaving that body in the car.'

He bent down and hoisted Edgar Cassidy to his shoulder.

'Come with me,' he snapped to Denise. 'I may need your help. I'll have some pretty stories to tell Davis and the servants in the morning. They'll notice Hester Coyne has gone. But the servants are under the impression that I'm a crazy fool dealing with criminals for some cranky reason. They don't worry when they see their pay packets.'

Paget dragged Edgar down to the car in which Marian Smith lay murdered. He placed the unconscious Edgar in the front seat and climbed in beside the steering wheel.

'You can do what the devil you like, Denise, but I have the feeling you'll be waiting for me when I return. I'm driving this ghastly load to town. What a fiendish way to spend a night! But it's got to be done. I know a man who'll get rid of the girl and the car.'

'I don't know why you get into the

racket,' grumbled Denise.

'Do you think I like this? I tell you I need money, and Lena Spelb is planning to open out in a big way. You don't realise the money there is in the game. Every big industrial city has its possibilities. Lena has agents everywhere. And she's got no scruples in gaining her objective.'

'I think she is an inhuman witch,' retorted Denise Hansen.

'I see you detest her, like most feminine women.' Paget took out some cigarettes, offered one to Denise, who was outside the car. He lit his cigarette and inhaled deeply. It seemed he needed the smoke badly. 'Well, I'm going.' He pressed the self-starter and the engine purred. 'Not a bad car for a newspaper reporter!'

He drove along the road, realising he was due for a grim hour because of Lena Spelb's viciousness. He gloated as he thought how he had fooled Edgar Cassidy with the dummy. That waxwork had been presented to Paget by the crazy designer of a waxwork show when Paget had refused to allow him to exhibit the dummy. Floyd Paget had guessed Edgar would return. His first idea had been to trap the reporter by using the dummy as a decoy. Denise Hansen's unexpected appearance had complicated the issue.

He thought about Denise. She was a nuisance. He wondered why she didn't realise she was standing on the brink of Hades itself. Foolish woman! He would have to get rid of her, and the best way was to send her to Lena Spelb. He drove on to town, dumping Edgar in a ditch en route. He had thought about killing the man, but on second thoughts it seemed stupid. Newspapers could raise the very dickens of a row, and it might be well-known in the office that Edgar Cassidy had gone down to see Floyd Paget at Wilderhouse.

He was leaving alive a real enemy. But the risk was not so great as it seemed. Edgar Cassidy could not collect any real proof of Paget's criminal activities at Wilderhouse. There remained only this dead woman, Marian Smith, and soon she would be disposed of along with Cassidy's car.

He drove along dark, deserted streets, to a disreputable riverside district.

6

Hester's Ordeal

Hester Coyne sprawled in the back of Lena Spelb's big car and struggled with the adhesive tape that bound her wrists. Four or five lashings of the strong tape were sufficient to clamp her hands together cruelly. She could not shout because a pad covered her mouth, fixed with the same adhesive tape.

Lena Spelb drove swiftly and efficiently. Soon it was obvious to Hester that they were heading for London. They passed through respectable suburban areas, which housed people who little realised that well-nigh incredible things could pass them in the night. Then into the broad, deeper streets of the city, Lena Spelb drove. Hester was wondering if she could attract attention when Lena turned suddenly from the main road and drove quickly through innumerable minor thoroughfares. It seemed to Hester — a country girl at heart who still knew little of the big city — that the streets were darker and almost deserted of people. At last, they came to the river. Hester caught a brief glimpse of the black waters and the shipping lights; then Lena Spelb turned the car again.

Finally the car turned into the incredible gloom of a viaduct tunnel. At the end it swung again and crawled into a dark, cobbled courtyard. Lena Spelb stopped the engine and climbed out. She came instantly to the rear door, opened it and gripped Hester's arm.

'Get out. You're going with me — out of sight! Hurry up — I want to get the car hidden. It doesn't pay to attract attention.'

Like some Frankenstein monster, Lena Spelb loomed head and shoulders over Hester. Her harsh-drawn face showed like a white mask in the gloom. She propelled Hester towards a door. She rapped four times in a peculiar way. With a strange suddenness the door jerked open, but there was no one to be seen behind it until Hester was pushed into the dark passage and then she saw a mulatto girl standing flat against the wall, holding the door.

Hester was guided down a narrow staircase that descended steeply. Hester Coyne's limbs were trembling at the thought of the horrors that lay ahead. That she was being taken into some ghastly house, or, perhaps, Lena Spelb's headquarters, she could not doubt.

So much for Floyd Paget's fine promises of an excellent job as his private secretary! It was to be hoped that no one else would follow the same path, Hester thought. The stairs terminated in a long, twisting passage, which was studded with doors. There was evidently an underground warren. The place was suffocatingly musty. Lena Spelb took her along with a firm grip, and there was nothing Hester could do but follow because she was so weak owing to the drug.

They passed a door when an ear-splitting shriek sounded from some dim recess behind. A second later Hester half-turned in fright as the door was wrenched open and a man and a dishevelled woman dashed into the passage. Screams came from the woman — screams of fear. The man who followed her seemed crazy. He snarled like an animal. He caught hold of the woman before she had gone many yards and began to strangle her. To Hester's nostrils drifted the peculiar acrid smell of Marihuana cigarettes, though she did not recognise it as such. She was too horrified to think clearly. She did not realise, also, that the Marihuana cigarettes had been smoked by the woman, because the thin little cylinders made horror easier to bear — for the moment.

Lena Spelb left Hester and strode over to the crazed man. She jerked him away and then hit him like a man. It was a strong blow that sent the man reeling to the ground. He crashed and lay still. Lena Spelb shouted along the passage. 'Danny!'

Her harsh tones brought a man shuffling from round a bend in the passage. He did not need any bidding, but picked up the prone man and carried him along the passage out of sight. Lena

214

Spelb grasped the woman and practically threw her back into the room. She closed the door and turned to Hester.

Hester felt like swooning with sheer dread of the unknown. Lena Spelb noticed her expression and she smiled. The smile was not reassuring. It was a mere twisting of the large, coarse face.

Hester trembled. She was using all her moral courage to stand firm. She told herself fervently that Lena Spelb's scheme couldn't happen to her.

'In here,' said Lena Spelb, and Hester was firmly directed towards a door which seemed dreadfully like the other compartments.

The room inside was obviously a cell. It had no windows and the electric light came from an unshaded bulb. A grimy bed stood in one corner. Hester eyed it with a shudder. A table and chair comprised the remaining furnishings. The floorboards were bare and dirty.

Lena Spelb whipped the adhesive tape from Hester's face and the pad fell to the floor. Hester's eyes smarted as the tape was jerked from her face, Lena Spelb smiled sardonically.

'We'll polish you up tomorrow and those red marks on your face will soon disappear. Have a cigarette, my dear.'

The Mistress of the Horrible extracted a cigarette from a case she carried in her slim handbag. She stuck the cigarette in Hester's mouth. She flicked on a lighter and held it for Hester.

After the first two draws Hester guessed the truth. The smoke was acrid. She instinctively spat out the cigarette.

'Don't you like Marihuana cigarettes?' drawled Lena Spelb.

'I hate everything about you! You've got to let me out! You can't keep me here!' Now that Hester could speak, her thoughts poured out in a torrent of words. 'You'll find you're making a mistake . . . Edgar Cassidy will discover you . . . I'm sure he will . . . I don't want your filthy cigarettes!'

'You will want them some day; you'll be glad of them. Don't worry. I believe Floyd Paget is taking care of Mr. Cassidy. At any rate, he could never find you in a million streets.'

'Where is Marian Smith?'

Lena Spelb looked angry; the incredible creature was angry with herself.

'I killed her. I was a fool. Why couldn't she be quiet? I could have used her.'

Hester shrank back. Lena regained her self-possession.

'Later you will be given something to eat. You needn't shout, because this place is underground. It is run for me by a figurehead,' Lena said strangely. 'We've had a long run. The police haven't even made an enquiry yet. Get some sleep, my dear. I don't want you to age overnight.'

Left by herself, Hester struggled for some time to loosen her wrists.

But the tape was unyielding. Finally she subsided on the wooden chair.

It seemed oppressively warm inside the room, and no doubt this was due to the lack of ventilation. Probably there was some method of circulating air in this underground warren, otherwise she visualised suffocation as her lot.

Hester was just an ordinary girl swept up in a bizarre series of events. The only mistake she'd made — and it was a human one — was to take up a job in such a lonely house as Wilderhouse. Now, from that prosaic start, she was incarcerated in a filthy hovel run by a travesty of a woman. It was a place where unimaginable events could happen.

After an hour the mulatto servant girl brought in a tray of food. She set it down on the table. Hester was surprised by its apparent quality. There was a pot of tea with milk and sugar and a little pile of canned meat sandwiches. They were on a spotlessly clean plate. On another plate lay some good biscuits.

'You have to drink,' said the girl in cockney English. She was a mere slip of a child with a dull expression. Her black hair hung lankly.

A faded kimono hung on her childish form. Her brown eyes stared blankly at the tray.

Hester thought of a desperate move.

'Untie my hands. I can't drink tea with my hands tied.'

For all the response she gave, the servant girl might have been deaf. Her dull eyes stared at the tray, and then slowly the girl poured out tea and added milk and sugar. She held the cup to Hester. For a moment Hester thought of dashing herself against the girl, knocking her down and escaping into the passage. But it didn't seem possible that such a simple act would enable her to get far. There would be guards. She would be intercepted, even if she could open doors with her hands tied behind her back.

Realising the tea might stimulate her courage, she drank from the cup the servant girl held. The tea was fresh and hot. It did her good.

'Can you get me out? I could get you some money . . . ' Hester's urgent appeal faded away when she saw a complete lack of response in the girl's eyes. The girl slowly shook her head, swinging it like a pendulum for a dozen times. She picked up a sandwich and held it for Hester to eat.

The meal was interrupted by the arrival of Lena Spelb. She entered the room in a hurry and brushed aside the servant girl. The girl shrank away, only to be recalled by Lena Spelb's harsh voice.'

'Help me with Hester. Get a cloth and clean her face. She's going over to the show. Hurry!'

Lena Spelb had brought a small, patent leather hatbox with her, but when she lifted the lid, Hester observed a heap of cosmetics and some pieces of finery. The servant girl came running with a bowl of water and a piece of cloth. Lena Spelb took the cloth impatiently and dabbed at the adhesive tape marks on Hester's face.

Hester felt a thrill of fear. Was this a prelude to some ghastly experience? She began to struggle. Lena Spelb called out: 'Mary, get hold of Danny.'

The servant girl hurried off obediently.

Despite Hester's struggles and kicks, Lena Spelb cleaned the girl's face. Then the girl returned with Danny. He was a lanky shuffling man in his forties. He had a deadpan, face and yellowish eyes. Lena spoke to him briskly.

'She's going over to the show, Danny. She's got to be dressed here. I'm in a devil of a hurry. She's got to take the place of one of the girls who killed herself an hour ago. It's a good show and I've got to have a girl with class. Take that tape off her wrists, Danny.'

Danny picked at the knotted ends of the tape. Within a minute he had the bindings off. It was a signal for Hester to struggle fiercely. But Danny gripped her arms until she cried out with the pain. She could scarcely move. Lena Spelb began to remove Hester's blouse with deft movements.

'Give me your word you'll not struggle and I'll send Danny away,' she leered. 'You see how considerate I am! You've got to get into these show clothes.'

Hester choked and nodded her head. She wondered why she didn't faint from stark fear. She stood limply while Danny went out of the door with an expressionless face. In the next five minutes Hester suffered Lena Spelb to effect a transformation. She was stripped and forced to don show clothes. They were of a cheap, filmy material, which would probably show vividly under a coloured limelight. Tight bands held the three filmy garments to her body. She was powdered effectively by Lena Spelb who seemed to be skilled in the procedure. Hester was transformed from a healthy English girl to a painted dancing-girl with a decided Oriental appearance. Lipstick was applied heavily to her lips, and her eyelashes daubed with mascara. Deftly Lena Spelb transformed her dark hair into a sophisticated coiffure. Finally sandals were fitted to her feet.

Hester stood swaying, her eyes closed. Her imagination conjured frightful possibilities. What dreadful scheme was this? Lena Spelb seemed to read the girl's thoughts.

'You've got nothing to worry about,' she said harshly. 'We just want you to stand in a tableau. I wouldn't use you, but a girl took some poison an hour ago — silly fool!'

To Hester it seemed there might be a chance of escape so she suffered herself to be led forward. They went into the passage, and Hester's cheeks burned under the powder and paint as she passed Danny standing beside the door. But the man's only expression was a flick of his yellowish eyes.

Once more Hester was taken to Lena Spelb's big car. She was given a wrap, which the servant girl brought, and Hester stepped into the rear seat with an inward shiver. Danny followed and shocked Hester by climbing into the rear seat beside her. Lena went to the wheel, and gave a mocking glance at Hester.

'Danny will see that you don't jump out, my dear. Don't worry, he has been in charge of more women than King Solomon and, anyway, he's got his orders.'

7

Edgar Finds an Ally

Edgar Cassidy groaned. He moved mostly because of reaction and with little deliberation. His mouth seemed to be full of mud. He spat chokingly. Then he sat up, holding his aching head. He was in a ditch and saw a half-moon shedding pale light over a deserted country lane. He was numb with cold and his feet were lying in six inches of chilly water. With an effort he clutched at the grassy bank and hauled himself to the dry road. He sat, running his hands through his hair, groaning while a flood of memories jarred into his mind.

Hester! That screaming fool of a woman . . . Paget and the insane dummy smiling into a fire . . . He'd been mad to allow that double-crosser Denise, to come with him to the house . . .

Edgar jerked to his feet. He remembered snatches of Denise Hansen's words

. . . She'd tried to trick him . . . tried to pretend she'd wanted to kill Floyd Paget . . . and Paget had sent Hester to Lena Spelb, the monster woman.

Edgar started to run down the road until he slowed with a bitter laugh at his wildness. He didn't know where he was. He might be anywhere. He'd lost his hat. What the blazes did that matter, anyway? He'd have to do something — quick. Could he hit on something that would lead to Hester? He began to run again. His circulation felt better as the blood pumped faster round his body. Edgar shoved a hand in his overcoat pocket. He felt for the gun, but he could not find it.

He'd kill Paget! No! He'd half-kill the man and then force him to reveal where he'd sent Hester. That was the only way. To go to the police meant answering too many questions . . . too much delay . . . too little personal action. At the moment he had one bitter, savage desire and that was to get his hands on the two people who had sent Hester Coyne to a living hell.

He wasn't an impressionable fool

— but when a man met a girl in a million, well, reckon out the odds. How many men meet girls like that? How many men pick up diamonds among glass?

Going to the police meant a search of London's dives. Lena Spelb had hidden from the police for a good many months now. As a newspaperman he'd heard about her. Searching for Lena would be like looking for the proverbial needle in the haystack.

In the meantime he had to reach civilization, and get a taxi if possible. Then return to Wilderhouse. He ran on and on. Edgar was lucky, On the point of exhaustion, he reached a small village. New life surged into his aching limbs. He passed a church and some locked-up shops and quiet houses and then came to the inevitable village pub.

He walked into the *Green Duck* creating a small sensation. Mine host, spotless behind his counter, blinked at Edgar's mud-coated appearance, his grimy face and generally dishevelled look. Edgar walked round the group of villagers who turned and eyed him candidly. He went to a vacant spot at the bar counter, and something about his manner brought the innkeeper towards him.

'What's wrong, son?'

'I'm a newspaper reporter. I ran into trouble. All I want is a drink and a car or a taxi. Can you tell me where to get a car?'

Edgar showed mine host his credentials. The *Daily Picture* was a popular newspaper and had graced the bar counter daily. The landlord studied the credentials with tantalising slowness, but Edgar knew better than to hurry a countryman. Finally mine host slowly pushed back Edgar's papers and sighed.

'Queer goings on there be nowadays.' He waddled across to the whisky and after measuring a double, brought it over to Edgar.

Edgar had not stipulated whisky. He grinned thinly. The landlord was a good judge of human nature. Edgar drank quickly, and brought out a note in payment.

'If you want a car,' said the landlord calmly, 'I've got one, but you'll have to

227

take my Bert along with you and pay him ten shillings and a pound for the car. I don't want my car damaged. Bert'll drive.'

'Who is Bert?'

'My boy. He's just left the army — them parachuters.'

'How far off is Wilderhouse?'

'Wilderhouse?' The landlord shook his head for an appreciable time. ' 'Taint in these parts. Never heard the name. Is it a village?'

'It's a house — belongs to Mr. Floyd Paget. I want to get there.'

'Bert'll know.' The landlord shuffled off to seek his son. 'I'll ask him.'

Edgar caught the eye of the girl behind the counter and ordered another whisky. He drank it appreciatively and felt hungry. He asked for sandwiches and got them. He had finished one before mine host reappeared with a tall cocky-looking fellow in corduroy trousers and sweater.

The landlord introduced: 'This is my lad — Bert.'

'Wilderhouse is nearly twelve miles away,' said Bert, 'though I'm not so sure I

228

know the house. Only heard today about Floyd Paget living there. If you hadn't mentioned his name . . . '

Edgar cut Bert short. He produced the necessary notes and laid them on the counter.

'I've got to get to Wilderhouse. It's a matter of life and death. Will you drive me over?'

Bert Latimer had had four years in the army and his judgment of men was quick and shrewd. He'd been a sergeant and had as many brains as the next man even if his childhood had been spent in a village pub. He saw in Edgar's grim eyes the battle light.

'I'll get the car out right away,' he promised. 'You can count on me.'

A few minutes later Edgar climbed into a dusty saloon. Bert Latimer had donned a leather jacket. Edgar clutched his sandwiches.

'Let's go,' said Edgar. 'Quick as mercury. I can tell you the details on the way, Bert. Incidentally, my name's Cassidy. Sometimes you can see it in the *Daily Picture*. Edgar Cassidy, that's my byline.'

'Glad to know you, chum.'

Bert shot the car away in a manner that showed he was no novice at driving. They tore up the road and out of the village, passing the ditch where Edgar had stirred to life.

Edgar did not want to give the impression he was mad, so he told the other the essentials of Hester's abduction, the murder of Marian Smith and Paget's scheme with Lena Spelb to elaborate the existing racket in dope dens and night clubs.

'This sounds like a good job,' said Bert.

'Good? What on earth is good about it? When I think of Hester — ' Edgar paused, murderously inclined.

'Well, it sounds like a spot of action,' said Bert apologetically. 'For the last few months I've felt browned-off pushing drinks across the old man's bar. It's hard to settle down, you know, after you've been demobbed, and another thing, chum — '

'You're supposed to drive,' commented Edgar grimly, not in the mood for small talk.

'You'll need a hand,' said Bert calmly. 'How the blazes does this Floyd Paget get away with it?'

The twelve miles to Wilderhouse were covered in fifteen minutes, which was remarkable speed in the night. Finally Edgar instructed Bert to park the car on a grassy patch off the road. As the car bumped over the grass, Edgar jumped out.

'I've got an appointment,' he said. 'Wait here.'

'I'm coming with you, chum.'

Edgar grinned, thinking of the woman who had entered Wilderhouse with him the last time. Denise Hansen had been a damned good actress, but he'd been a bigger fool to fall for her talk. Well, he knew he could count Bert.

'I won't refuse your help,' said Edgar. 'We've got a tough job.'

Tramping up the gravel drive seemed a little unreal. Lights were showing from windows in the big house. If it were not for the ache in his head, and the knowledge that Hester was probably in some horrible den, he would have thought he was back some five hours and approaching Wilderhouse for the first time. If that were the case, he'd be meeting a girl named Hester Coyne. She'd be sitting at a table, using it as a desk, in an outer room . . . Why the blazes was he thinking these futilities?

He was going to force Floyd Paget to reveal Hester's whereabouts! And if the man refused, he might not be responsible for his actions . . .

That was the difference five hours had made. Five hours! It seemed a lifetime. Edgar led Bert straight to the front entrance, and they tried the door. It was locked. Edgar thought of making a row, but that would put Paget on his guard. Then Edgar remembered the window, which opened easily. He beckoned Bert to follow him.

As he climbed through the downstairs window, he realised that this had happened before. Last time he had met Hester and there had been that thrillingly exciting moment in the stifling cupboard when he wanted to apologise but dared not speak too much in case Paget heard.

Now Hester was in the clutches of Lena Spelb, the monster woman.

Bert followed Edgar, and they moved into the passage in the manner of efficient housebreakers. Bert found himself thinking he should be carrying a rifle; instead he had to be content with bunching his capable fists. They entered the hall and moved across to the sitting room door. It seemed that Floyd Paget favoured this room more than his library. Edgar took a preliminary peep through the keyhole and saw there was light on the other side.

'This is it, Bert. What's the best technique?'

'Bust in, snap the light out and either dive for cover or rush the persons concerned,' whispered Bert promptly. 'After that — unarmed combat.'

'Straight from the textbook, eh? Okay.'

Edgar swung the door open and left Bert to knock up the switch. He had a photographic impression of Denise Hansen sitting near the fire writing a letter. She looked up, startled. Edgar gripped her after crossing the intervening carpeted floor in two seconds. He clamped his hand over her mouth, remembering that this was the woman who had previously double-crossed him.

'Where's Floyd Paget?' Edgar removed his hand for a second to allow her to reply.

'He's out!' She was about to shriek. Edgar clamped his hand over her mouth again. Bert came forward with a handkerchief, and with a wad of paper skilfully gagged the woman.

'This is the woman who tried to trick me,' said Edgar. 'I think she's something to Paget.' He bent down to examine the letter Denise Hansen had been writing.

It was an inconsequential script to some unknown man in London. Edgar dropped it on a table. He turned to Denise Hansen.

'Is Paget coming back tonight?'

She shook her head.

'You're lying,' snapped Edgar. 'You're waiting for him. You don't have to tell me.'

Bert found a cord holding some heavy curtains. He pulled the loose knot free, came over to the woman and bound her arms.

'When do we get hold of the man?' Bert asked. 'I'm not so easy doing this to a woman. Doesn't seem right.'

'Don't worry about that. It's a good guess that Denise is a menace to society.'

Edgar stood frowning. He felt a mass of indecision, and was irritated to feel that way. Thinking about Hester appalled him. He seemed further than ever from her. Here he was fooling about in Surrey and all the time Hester was miles away in London. If she was in Lena Spelb's hands she was sure to be in London, he felt.

'Well, he's not here,' said Bert quietly. 'What do we do now?'

Edgar felt he was at the bottom of a huge green sea and there was something unattainable at the top. He felt as miserable as a seal in the tropics. Then a snarling sound came from the drive. It was the sound of a car's engine. It coughed into comparative silence, and there was the banging of a door.

'Quick! Get Denise Hansen out of sight — behind that settee. Paget's coming!' Edgar's round, red face positively beamed with a mixture of savageness and glee. He leaped animatedly to help Bert with Denise Hansen. He was like a child who had been told to expect Father Christmas. They hid Denise and went to the door. Bert was about to switch off the light but Edgar interrupted him.

'If it is that swine, he might think it queer the light should cut off,' he said.

'Sorry, Edgar.' Bert gave a rueful grin. 'You think quicker than I do. My mind was on putting the room right from the inside.'

They stood behind the door. When it opened it would serve as an excellent shield from which to leap.

The door never opened.

The first sickening realisation that the plan had failed came to Edgar when a sharp sound made him spin round. He saw at the window a man with a gun. It was Floyd Paget, and he pushed the window frame open. It was the type that swung outwards like a door. The curtain was pushed to one side and Paget was crouched, wedged in the small gap. He steadied, pointing the revolver. There was no mistaking the deadly expression on his face. His lips were twisted in anger. Another second and he dropped into the room.

'You make mistakes like all of us, Cassidy. I saw the strange car. That was all that was needed to make me very cautious. The mistake I made was in allowing you to live. But that can soon be put right.'

Edgar eyed him sombrely.

'I see you have a companion, Cassidy,' said Paget. 'A pity. You see, I can't be lenient with either of you . . . Where is Denise?'

'She's gone,' said Edgar as if it didn't matter. 'She left when we arrived. It was merely an attempt to confuse his enemy.

'Another pity. I intended to dispose of Denise tonight and make a clean sweep of everybody standing in my way. Lena Spelb could take Denise where she wouldn't bother me any more.' Paget laughed thickly. 'Women — they make me sick! Lena Spelb is the only one who is an asset. Think of that, Mr. Cassidy. A surfeit of the creatures has brought me to that conclusion.'

'Where is Hester?' asked Edgar hoarsely.

'With our friend Lena. Pity I can't dispose of you so profitably.'

Paget strolled easily across his thick carpet, but his gun hand was as steady as if he were at revolver practice and his eyes never left his two captives. He stopped in front of the settee. He seemed to be considering.

The next moment the settee jerked as if propelled by power. The edge caught his legs at the back of the knees where the human limb can fold like a hinge. He staggered and his arms went down to his sides to break his fall . . . In split second reaction Edgar and Bert had flung themselves forward.

They did not have to be told that Denise Hansen had used her legs to fling the settee across the carpet. Coiled up, she had been able to use the full leverage of her limbs, and the settee had well-oiled castors. Hate and sudden fury had prompted her to crash the settee into the man who spoke so calmly of disposing of her.

Edgar was first to grab Paget. He landed with a crash that nearly broke the springs of the settee. The gun was lost in the fight that followed. Bert grabbed Paget's legs and stopped him from kicking savagely. Edgar leaned back and brought his fist crashing down into Paget's face. The man groaned. A thin trickle of blood came from his lips.

Bert found another cord. It came from the ornamental curtain that flanked the big bay window. Smaller curtains covered the glass panes. Bert looped the cord round Paget's threshing legs and bound them together. Then Bert went behind the settee and brought Denise Hansen into view He propped her in a chair beside Paget. Edgar was sitting on the man's chest.

Edgar hauled Paget up so that he could see the woman.

'That's where you went wrong, Paget. We all make mistakes.'

'You young swine!'

'To save a lot of trouble, I want to know where Lena Spelb has taken Hester.' Edgar held his fist ready. 'Now talk!'

'I haven't the slightest idea where she is.'

Edgar plunged his fist into the other's eyes. The man tried to avoid the blow, but he was unable to move quickly. He made a sobbing sound as pain shot through him. He tried desperately to throw Edgar from his chest. He tried to get his arm free from Edgar's left hand. His other arm was pinned under Edgar's thigh. Paget knew that a beating was coming to him, because, with Bert Latimer standing by, there was no possibility of escape.

Edgar continued with the grim task. He hammered the man and asked: 'Where's Hester?' He asked the question three times and struck the man after each question. Paget's mouth twisted in pain. His face was blotched with bruises and blood and he sucked in breath after each blow. Edgar's first anger had evaporated but he persisted grimly with the torture, hating the job. Then Paget's nerve cracked.

'You — you swine! Someday I'll make you pay for this — I'll remember how — '

'Where's Hester?' said Edgar sombrely.

'Lena Spelb — has her. There's a place on the river — Sine Street, Wapping. I hope she kills you!'

'Tie him up, Bert.'

It was the work of minutes because Paget was in a beaten condition.

'If you've lied, I'll come back and kill you,' said Edgar thickly.

They left Paget and Denise lying bound in the room. Edgar did not care greatly what happened to them. In his opinion the world would be well rid of such parasites as Denise Hansen and Floyd Paget.

Edgar and Bert ran to their car. Edgar wondered what had happened to his car and the corpse of poor Marian Smith. There wasn't time to waste in looking into the matter. A car with a corpse inside it was no use to him.

'Bert, I've got to make London quick. Can you take me there? Or will you trust me with the car? If anything happens to it I'll make it right with your old man.'

'And what if something happens to you?' Bert asked, as he pressed the self-starter. 'How do I make out then?'

'I'm pretty well insured. I'll make you out an I.O.U. if you like.'

'I was only kidding,' said Bert. 'I'm going all the way with you. This Lena Spelb seems a lousy piece of work.'

Bert sent the saloon rocking down the road in a positively dangerous manner.

Inside Wilderhouse, Floyd Paget managed to hobble to a bell, which he pressed, bringing the butler from his sleep in the soundproof basement.

8

Appointment with Death

Hester Coyne felt she was in a madhouse. She was standing on a dais motionless. A glaring limelight blinded her, flooded her in yellow light. She stared into an impenetrable area of darkness all round her, whilst round the base of the dais, in the circular pool of light girls danced and weaved.

The girls' postures were grotesque and frightening to the girl on the dais. So alien were they that she only dimly comprehended their meanings. There was a strange hush in the low-roofed hall. Hester knew that in the darkness people sat, a gloating audience. The darkness was not relieved. Light was not desired by the patrons of Lena Spelb's secret show except on the weird performers.

Hester stood rigid though every nerve in her body screamed that she should dash away. But she remembered Lena

Spelb's last words before they led her to the dais in the blinding gloom before the limelight revealed the scene.

'Do as you've been instructed or I'll send you to Li Su's — tonight!' Lena had told Hester.

Hester was placed between the evil she knew and the threat of worse horrors. The bizarre dance went on and on, a seemingly crazy performance that satisfied the sensation-jaded patrons. Hester closed her eyes and waited for the end.

In a dark, furtive passage that led to the square stage, Lena Spelb watched her latest offering. She seemed satisfied and turned to Danny.

'Bring the girl back to the riverside house when it's over. I'm going back there. I'll send another car over here in time to pick you up.'

The man nodded, his bulging eyes fixed on the show.

At Wilderhouse Floyd Paget was freed from the binding cord by Davis, his butler. The butler made many expressions of incredulity, though his attitude betrayed the fact that he had expected odd happenings for some reason or other. Paget muttered something about enemies and waved the man back to his room.

Denise Hansen had also been freed by the butler. She glared at Paget, remembering the fate he had outlined for her while she had been eavesdropping behind the settee.

'I'm going — you swine! I hope you get killed!' she panted,

He made as if to strike her, and then his eyes gleamed.

'I'm going after that young fool,' he said. 'I'll need your car. Apparently you've placed it in the garage. Did you intend to stay? I came back from town in a hired car, but the man has gone. Your small car will do because mine might attract too much attention where I'm going.'

Ten minutes later Paget was driving through the night — for an appointment with death.

* ★ *

Edgar Cassidy and Bert Latimer hunched in their seats as the car trundled through the darker streets of Wapping dock. They were looking for Sine Street, and even Edgar with his knowledge of London districts was at a loss.

They stopped to question a few individuals from time to time. Once their car passed two policemen who patrolled in pairs because danger lurked in the shadows.

'What about getting those two coppers on the job?' asked Bert.

Edgar shook his head.

'I admire the police, but some of them can be deucedly hard-headed . . . With half a break we'll get results while the police are asking questions and writing down the answers in a notebook.'

They questioned a few more passersby. Mostly they were men who wore mufflers and shapeless felt hat. They all looked furtive. They mumbled a lot. One stared and stepped quickly into an unlighted alley, not answering. But finally one chuckled whiningly.

'Sine Street? I'll take you to the joint guv'nor, for the price of a few drinks.'

Edgar opened the car door for him.

They crawled along the road, and the weedy specimen gave instructions. Edgar pressed two silver coins into his warm, smelly hand. 'Another two when we get there,' Edgar promised.

They had a few cobbled, twisting streets to traverse, with streetlamps few and far between. Then their guide coughed: 'Sine Street, guv'nor.'

Bert dimmed the headlights. The alley seemed to jut on to an incredibly black tunnel. Edgar said:

'Have you ever heard of a woman called Lena Spelb?'

The guide merely made an inarticulate frightened noise.

'Just which door do we tackle to get to her?' Edgar pressed. 'Could you do with a pound?'

The man grabbed the note.

'The first door before the tunnel, guv'nor. I wouldn't go in there if I were you. I hear she's got some dangerous hard cases working for her. Gawd! Lemme get out! I didn't oughter 'ave split on Lena.'

The guide disappeared, mumbling into the darkness.

'Turn all the car lights off, Bert,' said Edgar. 'Do you feel like it now?'

'You bet. Let's get cracking.'

'I don't know how I can repay you — '

'We haven't started yet,' was Bert's rejoinder. 'How do you know I won't get the wind up?'

'You won't,' said Edgar warmly.

They walked to the door that was set in a small courtyard. There seemed to be a deep, sound-proofing darkness lying over the whole place. They stood close to the door and then a moment later they dashed round a projecting corner as a car engine sounded softly in the road.

The car was big and black and made so little noise that it might have been pushed into the courtyard. Bert and Edgar, behind the irregular shaped wall, dared not look from their hiding-place because the car's headlights were illuminating the whole courtyard. They heard a door bang and guessed someone was stepping out of the car. Then the car's lights went out. Edgar chanced a look round the wall, and hastily summoned Bert to follow him.

Edgar ran over the cobbles with the swiftness of a native runner. His impetus carried him on to the back of a tall, female figure and they both crashed to the ground before Lena Spelb could knock four times on the door. Edgar gripped the woman by the throat, choking off any cry for help. He dragged her round the projecting wall to the corner of the yard. For a minute he nearly choked the woman, while her arms threshed wildly at his wrists, gouging flesh and blood. Bert stood by warily.

'I want Hester Coyne,' insisted Edgar. He eased his grip a little. 'Is she somewhere in this dump?'

Lena Spelb struggled fiendishly. The respite given her was used to gulp air and claw at Edgar's face. She had the strength of a man with the wildcat nature of a desperately evil woman.

For the second time Edgar nearly strangled her, and this badly scared Lena Spelb. She began to talk hoarsely, spitting out words.

'The girl is in a show . . . It'll break her spirit . . .'

Edgar punched her cruelly in the side. She writhed.

'You . . . can . . . have her . . . What is one girl . . . ? Aaah! You'll kill me, you fool!'

'I'll certainly kill you if I don't find Hester Coyne . . . Where is this show?'

'A mile away.'

'Get in the car,' ordered Edgar. He let the woman rise to her feet, and he held her arm. He held it in such a manner that one jerk would dislocate it agonisingly. Bert jumped forward and caught her other arm.

They got into the car with difficulty, and Bert started the engine. He backed the car out of the courtyard in a few seconds. Edgar was having a savage time with the half-mad Lena Spelb. He quieted her with a quick blow to the face. She subsided. Bert was slowly driving along the road. Lena Spelb revived and tried to fight again. Edgar forced himself to hit her twice. He felt disgusted with himself, but justified his action with the thought that she deserved worse. Lena Spelb fell back, moaning harshly.

'Which way?' asked Edgar. 'If you're tricking us . . . '

'To hell with you! You can have her. I'll show you the way. I value my life . . . more than . . . your blasted woman.'

Bert waited. Lena Spelb found more breath and spat blood.

'Straight along this road . . . then Santoy Road . . . I'll show you after that . . . '

The car gathered speed.

★ ★ ★

Floyd Paget drove like a maniac. Denise Hansen's car had a good turn of speed, though on a straight main road its maximum speed could not be considered dangerous.

He was obsessed with the idea of catching up with Edgar and his companion. They had merely a few minutes start: perhaps ten minutes had elapsed before Davis answered the persistently-ringing bell and released his employer from the bonds.

Paget carried a revolver. He had found

his weapon kicked under some furniture. If he once caught up with Cassidy's car, he would shoot them as he passed and risk the resultant investigations.

Paget crammed on more speed. He took bend after bend recklessly, reluctant to slow down for a few seconds.

The end came when an acute hairpin bend loomed up in the dark. His speed was too great for even a racing motorist. He realised it too late, his lust for speed dropping from him in sheer terror as he frantically strove to slow it down for a few seconds.

The sports car rocked and slithered. It slid halfway round the bend with a frightful jarring of metals and screaming tyres. The engine still lunged powerfully and the drubbing wheels rocketed the car straight towards a gaunt telegraph post.

The car crashed deafeningly and buckled up. The man inside splayed forward through the jagged windscreen and became wedged horribly

Paget lay like that and died slowly . . . painfully.

Hester Coyne was suddenly aware that the blinding light had died away. She opened her eyes and the velvet darkness pressed all around her Then she heard scampering sounds all around and realised the girls were running down the dark aisle.

Suddenly a hand grasped her arm. It was a hard, rough hand. She knew instinctively it belonged to Danny. He led her away, finding the aisle unerringly though Hester could not distinguish anything in the gloom. She heard a low murmur of voices on all sides and then her eyes became accustomed slightly to the dark and she perceived red, glowing lights, which were cigarette and cigar ends.

As Hester shrank in horror there was a hubbub at the extreme end of the passage. A thunderous crash sounded on the door. Hester wheeled. In the indistinct light she saw three people advancing. They seemed so hazy, so unreal that she thought she was having mad dreams. Then she screamed.

She saw Lena Spelb flanked by two young men. One of the men was Edgar Cassidy, unless she was crazy with delusions. The two men were dragging Lena Spelb. They approached swiftly, like curious green figures in a dream. The next moment there was a fierce uproar. Danny tried to drag Hester away, but she fought like a fiend seeing an escape from doom. One of the young men turned and knocked Lena Spelb to the ground.

The next instant Edgar's voice was real and invigorating. She could have sobbed with relief.

Danny let go of Hester. His hand rammed into a pocket as Edgar closed with him ready to kill. Edgar beat the man by slamming two fists into his stomach. Then he saw the gun. Danny was drawing it from his pocket. Edgar kicked it from his hand and grabbed the man's neck. They fell against the wall, and Edgar seized the opportunity to crash the man's skull against the wall. He did it twice, feeling that boxing rules were distinctly out of place at the moment.

He picked up the revolver and swept

round to Hester, aghast at her exotic make-up.

'Hester! Thank heavens I've found you. What in mercy's name have they done to you? We've a chance to get out of here! But hurry!'

Men were running. Edgar almost carried Hester down the passage. Then they had trouble with a doorman. He was huge, but Bert tackled him without hesitation. As they forced their way to the door, four men came running down the passage and in the middle was Lena Spelb, her face working. In her hand was a levelled gun.

A bullet whined past Edgar's head, smacking into the doorjamb with a splintering impact.

Instinctively, Edgar turned and fired into the mob.

He pressed the trigger four times rapidly. There was a hoarse roar of pain from one man. The others scampered to doorways. They left a tall figure in black slowly sinking to the ground, still holding a smoking gun.

It was Lena Spelb. Edgar caught one

last glimpse of her as he hustled through the door. Before him he smelled sweet night air and freedom. Behind him he left a dying woman — but a woman in whom evil had run rampant.

One of the four bullets had entered Lena's body.

Edgar carried Hester out to the car where he found a rug and tenderly put it round her scantily-clad form.

* * *

Edgar Cassidy was dressed to impress. His tweed suit seemed pretty good, his hair was oiled and he had bought a new car. 'Gosh, Hester, this car is a good one!'

She felt the leather upholstery. Edgar took his eyes from the road to watch her.

'Do you like it?' he asked.

'I do,' she smiled.

'Do you like the weather? Smashing, isn't it?'

'Yes, I like the weather. Give me sun and light — always,' she said.

'You like my new car and you like the weather I provide,' said Edgar calmly.

'The question now is: do you like me?'

She said rapidly: 'I should think the question should be a statement of intentions.'

He stopped the car.

'Look here, Hester, I've got to tell you someday, so it may as well be now. I love you. When I thought I'd lost you, I got grey hairs. There, it's out. I wonder what you'll say!'

She came very close to him.

'I can only say you've waited so long that I thought you'd changed your mind. But I suppose you were only waiting until the police investigation was over . . . and until I got over that awful affair . . . Kiss me, you idiot!'

THE END